The Fledglings

Max Hennessy was the pen-name of John Harris. He had a wide variety of jobs from sailor to cartoonist and became a highly inventive, versatile writer. In addition to crime fiction, Hennessy was a master of the war novel and drew heavily on his experiences in both the navy and air force, serving in the Second World War. His novels reflect the reality of war mixed with a heavy dose of conflict and adventure.

Also by Max Hennessy

The RAF Trilogy

The Bright Blue Sky
The Challenging Heights
Once More the Hawks

The Captain Kelly Maguire Trilogy

The Lion at Sea
The Dangerous Years
Back to Battle

The Flying Ace Thrillers

The Mustering of the Hawks
The Mercenaries
The Courtney Entry

The Martin Falconer Thrillers

The Fledglings
The Professionals
The Victors
The Interceptors
The Revolutionaries

The
FLEDGLINGS

JOHN HARRIS WRITING AS
MAX HENNESSY

🔟 CANELO

First published in the United Kingdom in 1971 by Hutchinson Junior Books Ltd

This edition published in the United Kingdom in 2020 by

Canelo

31 Helen Road

Oxford OX2 0DF

United Kingdom

A CIP catalogue record for this book is available from the British Library.

Print ISBN 978 1 80032 737 5

Ebook ISBN 978 1 80032 078 9

Look for more great books at www.canelo.co

Printed and bound in Great Britain by Clays Ltd, Elcograf S.p.A.

1

Chapter 1

That spring of 1915, the first of the war, there appeared to be a scarcity of duck and as we crouched in the punt under the steely Norfolk sky we were all a little discouraged. They said that, with the fighting making food scarce, there was a lot of poaching going on and, certainly, we often saw men moving across the marshes near Fynling with what could easily have been guns under their coats.

The Widdows girls had decided it was far too cold to squat in a punt and watch the three of us trying to find something to shoot at and they'd decided to stay at home and help Mother get a meal ready for when we returned. And now, with nothing to see and nothing to shoot at, we were beginning to wish we'd stayed with them.

I looked across at Frank – Frank Griffiths – who was already grey-faced and red-nosed with the cold, crouching under an oilskin, his hands blue, his expression thoroughly disillusioned. Frank was at school with me, but he came from inland Leicester – about as far from the sea and the Norfolk marshes as you could get – and though he'd said he fancied doing a bit of shooting when we came home on holiday, in fact I think he was already beginning to decide he was much happier around the busy shopping streets of Norwich.

Even my brother, Geoffrey Falconer, at the other end of the punt, looked as though he'd lost interest. He'd gone after duck with me ever since I'd been able to hold a gun, but this time he'd been a little indifferent.

I shivered in the damp salty breeze and glanced across at him. He was taller than I was, fair in the romantic faraway-eyed manner of a poet, with a long curving lock that persisted in hanging over his right eye. He was actually tougher than he looked, but he'd always had this out-of-this-world look about him and at the moment it was more marked than ever.

As I studied him, he shifted his position slightly in the boat, easing the stiff leg he'd brought back from France, and I could tell from his expression that he was thinking about anything but duck. I'd never been sure – not even from the minute I was old enough to be aware of him – what was in his mind because he was always more impractical than I was and inclined to drift off into daydreams;

but while he couldn't mend a broken bicycle, the thoughts that sometimes raced through his head left me standing, never quite certain what he meant, his attitudes deep-rooted in sensitivity and intelligence of a sort that I couldn't hope to emulate.

He hadn't particularly wanted to go shooting – 'I've had enough shooting for a while,' he'd said – and Frank was the one who'd persuaded him. While I might simply not have bothered to chivvy him, Frank had tormented him and pulled his leg until he had finally agreed. But his heart had not seemed in it from the beginning, and when we found nothing, I could see his thoughts had drifted away to something else entirely and he was completely unconcerned now whether we got a shot or not.

For a man who found so much interest in life this casualness worried me. Geoffrey was interested in everything – what made people do what they did, how they thought, the colours of the sky over the marshes in the evening, and the way the frost gathered on the willows in the winter. He was always the first to notice that the swallows had arrived and the first to see the immediate signs of autumn, things that for the most part passed me by.

I could dismantle a motor-bike without the slightest difficulty but I could never keep up with Geoffrey, and his manner at the moment worried me.

Despite his romanticism, his out-of-the-worldness, it was quite unlike him, but he'd been pretty indifferent to what went on ever since he'd come home from France. He was three years older than I was and already considering university when the war had broken out, but, like so many others, instead of following the pursuits of peacetime, he'd gone off in a rush of patriotism to join the Army. At first, like all his friends, he'd not believed that Kitchener's appeal, *Your Country Needs You,* had applied to him. We weren't of the class that normally supplied private soldiers for the Army, yet we also weren't of the class that supplied the officers either. But then, as the retreat from Mons had started and the French countryside had filled with the dragging dusty figures of British troops and all those men we'd seen off to war not long before with cheers and waving flags had found themselves fighting for their lives, it had dawned on Geoffrey and all his contemporaries that Kitchener had meant *them* after all – not the men standing behind them. That pointing finger and staring eyes were directed at them, not the men on the next corner, and he had gone off in a rush, his mind full of fervour and his talk studded with quotations which indicated that he believed it was right and fitting to die for his country.

He'd been wounded on the first day of the Battle of Neuve Chapelle – not seriously, but enough to guarantee him a long rest in England – and, still limping a little from the fragment of metal through his thigh, I had an idea he wasn't looking forward to going back. Somehow he'd changed beyond all recognition. All those romantic quotations that had filled his conversation had vanished abruptly and the eager light of a martyr that had been in his eye had faded. He was paler than he had been and was suddenly more terse in speech after his six months in France. Sometimes, even, his tongue had an unexpected sharp edge to it, but, in spite of this, he was also much quieter and introspective than he'd been before the war and had taken to going for long walks by himself and – recently – with Edith Widdows.

We'd known the Widdows family most of our lives. I'd taught Edith to play tennis; I'd played cricket with her, swum with her on Yarmouth beach; gone to the circus with her at Christmas, unwillingly dragging her younger sister Jane with us. Even gone to see the man who'd brought a strange box-kite-like contraption to a field outside Norwich in 1912 and made it fly, buzzing over our heads like a sewing machine running wild.

Edith was eighteen now, eighteen months older than I was, quiet, intelligent, and perfect to spend a day with – when we could get away from Jane, who was fifteen by this time and far too big for her boots.

I'd met Edith first when we'd moved to the house at Fynling near Wroxham. Her father farmed the land around and it was Edith who'd taught me to sail and her father who'd first taken me with him in a punt after duck. He'd lent us a pony and trap occasionally, too, when ours was in use, and Jane – typical of Jane – had kept ferrets and showed me how to use them to bolt the rabbits from their holes. The families had drawn so close over the years, we almost lived in each other's laps. I never went home without finding one of the Widdowses in the kitchen talking to my mother, and I have no doubt that at times old Widdows, coming home from a tiring day in Norwich market, didn't always relish the sight of the two boys who were talking to his daughters with their feet up on his hearth.

'I think it's getting colder, Martin,' Frank said suddenly, breaking into my thoughts. 'This beastly wind's freezing.'

'You don't know what cold is,' I said. 'You ought to be here in January when the east wind's coming straight from Russia.'

'With snow on its boots,' Geoffrey added, and we grinned. We'd all heard the story that had gone the rounds in 1914 – that Russian troops had passed through England to help in the big attacks against the Germans in France. Someone had seen troops with snow on their feet, I'd heard, and with a bit of wishful thinking had made them into the first drafts of a vast Imperial Russian Army coming to help Gallant Little Belgium against the invader. The story had shot round England overnight, it seemed, until everyone had believed it.

'Come to think of it,' Geoffrey said, 'maybe it *is* time we went home. It'll be dark soon.'

'Another half-hour,' I suggested. 'We might still be lucky.'

Geoffrey stared at me, then he shook his head in a way that meant there would be no argument. Despite his dreaming, Geoffrey could be stubborn.

'There'll be a meal,' he said. 'And a fire. And some dry clothes.'

'You're getting soft, Geoffrey,' Frank smiled.

Geoffrey's gaze moved to Frank's grinning face. 'You think so?' he said.

'A meal. A fire. Dry clothes.' Frank gave an expansive gesture. 'You're getting to be an old woman.'

Geoffrey smiled at last, a smile that lit up his face. 'Not an old woman,' he said. 'An old soldier.'

I looked at him quickly. Geoffrey rarely talked about his time with the Army in France but he sometimes dropped little comments like this that gave me a clue to what it was like: cheerless, unwarmed, hungry, living in holes in the ground. It was a new idea of warfare to me. I'd always thought of war as men on horses waving flags, or charging against enemy fortifications. But all *that* seemed to have stopped very early in this war because it had been discovered very quickly that cavalry attacks weren't much good against riflemen behind fortifi-cations.

And the heavy guns that had been brought up to destroy the fortifications had only driven the defenders into the ground, and when the thwarted Germans had therefore tried to get round the ends of the trenches that had been dug to the north and the south, the trenches had been pushed still further north and south to stop them. Now they ran all the way from the coast to Switzerland – right across France. Two sets of them, with a narrow soured stretch of despoiled countryside between them, barred with barbed wire, fouled with rubbish and all the litter of war, and torn again and again by the high explosive that was flung into it before every new attempt to break a way through.

–

My mother and the girls had a meal waiting for us when we returned. Hot strong tea, pork pie and pickle, and thick slabs of toast dripping with butter to fill us up, and they hovered around us while we stuffed ourselves with it.

'Anybody would think you hadn't eaten for a month,' Jane said, staring at me filling my mouth.

Mother laughed. 'Perhaps they're taking precautions,' she said. 'They're back at school in two days.'

'So am I,' Jane said. 'Hallelujah, back to woollen stockings and brown gym slip.'

'We all have to suffer,' Frank grinned. 'Even Geoff's going back before long.'

I saw Mother and Edith exchange glances. They had always got on well together, those two, and particularly lately. My mother was a painter of some note and most of the time her affairs were a shambles because some idea would catch her mind just when she was busy about the house and she would have to drop everything to put it on to canvas. There had been many times when, in desperation, we'd gone across to the Widdowses' for a meal because Mother was busy slopping paint on in the studio at the top of the house and had forgotten all about us. Edith had a similar absorption with music and sat for hours playing Liszt or Chopin while I egged her on to play something a little more lively from the music halls that you could sing. Sometimes she obliged but mostly she would shake her head with a smile, as stubborn as Geoffrey when it pleased her to be.

Mother had turned away from the table as Frank had spoken and I saw her smile die.

'Yes,' she said quietly. 'Geoffrey's going back, too, before long.'

'I wish I were going with him,' Frank announced. 'I'm sick of waiting till I'm old enough to join up.'

'Thank your lucky stars you're *not* old enough,' Geoffrey said, his head bent over his plate, and my mother turned away quickly and went into the kitchen.

We were all staring at Geoffrey now.

'Well, gosh,' Frank said, 'everybody wants to get into the scrap, don't they?'

Geoffrey looked up. 'It's not a football match, Frank,' he said with a trace of that new sharpness in his voice. 'You don't call half-time after three-quarters of an hour, have a slice of lemon and a rest, and then start again. And when it's over you don't have a hot shower and go home to a good meal, with nothing worse than a few bruises. People sometimes get killed.'

Frank glanced at me, then turned back to Geof-frey, puzzled. Frank was an extrovert like me, not much of a scholar and enjoying games and cycling and, lately, the company of girls. He never had much difficulty finding them, either, because they fell at once for his dark curls and the lively look in his eye.

'But of course they do,' he was saying. 'There's a war on. That's what it's all about.'

Geoffrey looked angry, then Edith put a hand on his arm and I saw him calm down.

'Not quite,' he said more evenly. 'It isn't flags and trumpets these days, you know. War's a messy business and, for some, pretty painful and inglorious.'

It was unlike Geoffrey to talk like this. At school he'd been a superb athlete, quite indifferent to the knocks he'd received, always willing to take risks and quite unafraid of the odds against him.

'You were keen enough to get into it,' I reminded him, remembering the way he'd ridden off on his bicycle into Norwich within three weeks of the war starting. Already everybody had been seeing German spies everywhere and even elderly foreign governesses were being viewed with suspicion, and when the village cricket pavilion had burned down he'd seen the hand of German agents in it and rushed off to join up and avenge it.

He looked up at me, turning his head slowly. 'Yes,' he said. 'I was. That was before I knew anything about it. Things changed a bit during the winter. And even more after Neuve Chapelle. There's nothing so likely to knock the stuffing out of you as a wound.'

'Why?' Jane leaned forward, sitting astride a chair in a most unladylike way, her arms on the back, her dark plaits hanging over her wrists.

Geoffrey gestured. 'Up to then,' he said, 'you feel pretty brave, because you always think that you'll never get hit – that it'll always be the chap next to you. When you finally stop one, you begin to realise that *you* can get hurt, too, and you begin to realise that the chap lying out in front in the grass – still there after days because no one can get to him to fetch him in – might have been you.'

It was a long speech for Geoffrey – the longest he'd ever made on the subject of the war. But I don't think it convinced Frank. It certainly didn't convince me. I'd read too much in the newspapers about 'Our brave troops' and 'The glorious dead' and I still saw the war as Frank did, as an affair of slapping flags and colour and courage and the nobility of dying.

Geoffrey pushed his chair back and lit a cigarette – which was another difference I'd noticed in him. Before he'd joined the Army, he'd always thought smoking would destroy his wind for running. He hadn't drunk either, but I'd noticed, too, since he'd come home that he hadn't been against helping himself to Father's whisky. Mother had tried to stop him once, but my father, who'd served in the Yeomanry in the Boer War, shook his head and said nothing, as though he had some idea how Geoffrey felt. It was as though he almost hated the war.

It was an attitude which was very puzzling to me because at school all of us in the upper forms were only waiting until we could leave and demand commissions. And although I didn't think for a minute that Geoffrey was afraid, I thought perhaps he was tired or something and not seeing things quite as he ought.

'Never mind, Geoff,' I said. 'We'll look after you. We'll be joining you in the trenches soon.'

Geoffrey smiled. 'You won't be joining *me*, old son,' he said, 'because I'm not going back to the trenches.'

Frank grinned. 'What girls do to a chap,' he said.

'What girls?' I asked.

Frank glanced at us all in turn. 'Oh, just girls,' he said mysteriously.

I was still wondering what he meant when dreadful suspicions shot across my mind. I stared at Geoffrey. My jaw had dropped open.

'Geoff,' I said, 'you're not going to…?'

'Not going to what?'

I didn't know how to put it, I felt so ashamed of what I was thinking.

'I mean…' I blushed. 'Well, you're not going…?'

He suddenly saw what I was driving at and put the fear into words.

'Desert?' He gave a hoot of laughter. 'Not likely. It's just that I can't see much sense in living in a hole in the ground, having the Germans throw everything they've got at me, covered with mud and stinking like a polecat, when I can live like a gentleman in a clean billet and fight where the whole place's swept clean before the next set-to.'

Frank looked puzzled. 'Where's that?' he asked.

Geoffrey extended one finger and jerked it upwards several times. 'Up there,' he said. 'In the sky.'

Going to war in a flying machine had never occurred to me before. In fact, I didn't really believe that people did. I'd seen pictures of flimsy machines manoeuvring against each other and men firing across the intervening space with rifles or trying to drop apple-sized bombs or steel darts on the troops below. I'd even read in the paper about 'intrepid birdmen' and their 'death dives' but I wasn't very sure what a death dive was. Particularly as no one appeared to die as a result of them. And no one ever seemed to hit anything when they shot at each other. It didn't seem much like a war to me, floating about above the earth. From what I could make out, all they did was find out where the enemy was for the infantry below, with few chances of getting a shot at them because their machines were too vulnerable against ground fire.

'You mean you're transferring?' Frank asked.

Geoffrey smiled. 'Lots of chaps are doing it,' he said. 'They take you on trial and if you find you get on well together, you stay. If they don't like you or you don't like them, you go back to your regiment. But *I* shan't go back. I've made up my mind. That's the way to fight a war. No mud. No lice. No smells. They live like lords, sleep between sheets, and have a drink and a hot bath when they come back.'

'Do they *fight*?' Frank asked. 'I mean, properly.'

'Knights in armour,' Geoffrey said, still smiling. 'Man against man. Face to face. One machine against another. None of this business of sitting in a hole in the ground waiting for a chap five miles away to pull a trigger that'll drop a shell on you without him seeing you and without you seeing him.'

Frank turned to me. 'Ought to suit you, Martin,' he said. 'You're a good shot.'

Though I hadn't expected it to, it started a train of thought in my mind that I found I couldn't put aside. And the more I thought about it, the more interesting it seemed. I decided after supper to have a word with Geoffrey about it. It seemed a good opportunity because Jane had gone off with Frank on bicycles to the village, pleased to be with him as girls always seemed to be, and I was alone.

I found my mother in front of her easel, dressed in a paint-smudged smock, a long strand of hair hanging over her eyes.

'Where's Geoff?' I demanded.

She looked at me, her eyes vague, as though she didn't properly see me, then she seemed to switch on as she managed to thrust what had been occupying her thoughts from her mind.

'Gone to the Widdowses',' she said, swinging back to the easel.

'I'll catch him there.'

I hadn't realised she could move so fast. She had put down the palette and brush in one movement and grabbed my arm as I turned for the door.

'No,' she said, and all the absorption with her painting that had been in her eyes had gone at once. Abruptly, she was no longer a painter. She was my mother and she was giving the orders.

'Well, if he's there...' I began.

Her grip on my arm didn't loosen. 'He's doing something for Mr Widdows, I think,' she said. 'He won't want you.'

'What's he doing?'

She was a little uncertain. 'Helping with accounts or something.'

I didn't argue, because the two families often helped each other out, though I'd never heard before that old Widdows needed assistance with his accounts and Geoffrey was no great hand at arithmetic. Nevertheless, I decided to leave it until the next morning, but the next day, when I went downstairs, Mother announced that Geoffrey and Edith had gone to Norwich for the day to buy materials for Mrs Widdows.

'Oh, hell,' I said. 'There was something I wanted to ask him.'

My mother seemed suddenly more alert than normal. 'What?' she asked.

'Oh, nothing,' I said. 'Nothing important.'

She knew I was being cagey. 'Are you sure?'

'Yes. I'm sure. Nothing at all.'

Frank and I spent the day fishing, but it came to an abrupt end when Jane appeared and started wanting to help. Frank began to tease her about her clumsiness and in the end she gave him a violent furious shove so that he went into the water up to his waist and we set off home with him dripping water and squelching in his shoes, while Jane giggled and kept offering him one of the fish we'd caught because she said he looked just like a sea lion she'd once seen in a circus.

I had half expected Geoffrey and Edith to be back when we arrived but there was no sign of them and as they didn't appear until supper-time I didn't get any chance that day either. I decided I'd tell Edith what I thought of her when I got a chance, hogging Geoffrey like that. We'd always told each other exactly what we'd felt.

The next day we were due to leave for school and, as Edith and Mother seemed to be hanging round Geoffrey all the time, I still didn't get a chance to talk to him. But what he'd said had really started something in my mind that continued to nag at me, so that during the following term after Geoffrey had gone back to some rear-echelon unit in France until his leg was stronger, I told Frank that I was going to chuck school and join up.

We were punting a ball round on the playing fields at the time, and he slammed it at me and stood with his hands on his hips, grinning at me.

'Right,' he said immediately. 'I'll come with you. As soon as we're old enough.'

'We're almost seventeen,' I pointed out.

'You can't get a commission until you're eighteen.'

'You can in the Flying Corps,' I pointed out. 'They'll take you at seventeen if you're the right type. Youngsters are what they're after. Flying's a new thing and they want people with open minds, not old fogeys in their twenties.'

Frank looked interested. Like all the seniors at school, he resented still being treated as a boy when the most exciting thing that had ever happened in our lives was taking place just across the Channel.

'Honest?' he said.

'Honest. I wrote to a chap I know.'

'Geoffrey?'

I frowned. 'No. *He* just told me to stay where I was until they fetched me – and longer than that if I could. It was a chap from Norwich I know whose cousin's an observer.'

Frank considered the idea, his eyes gleaming. 'What do we do?' he asked. 'Put it to the headmaster?'

I shook my head. 'He might try to stop us. I think we should write straight to the War Office and see what they say.'

'All right.' His face was alight with enthusiasm. 'We'd better not mention our age at first, though, in case they think we're just kids. But we've got to sound keen. Is Geoff in yet?'

'Any time. He's due home from France to train as a pilot.'

Frank's eyes shone. 'Wouldn't it be terrific if they sent us to the same place as him?' he said.

We spent days over the letters, writing and rewriting them. Now that he'd been convinced, Frank's enthusiasm knew no bounds.

'We've got to sound adult and mature,' he said eagerly.

'But not too adult and mature to have lost all our youthful keenness,' I warned.

'That's right. Think we ought to address them as "Dear Sir" or just "Sir"?'

'What's the difference?'

'Well, "Sir" sounds more soldierly.'

'Sounds more like one of the juniors up before the Head. What's wrong with "Dear Sir"?'

'Can't have 'em thinking we're too affectionate,' Frank grinned.

We argued every word on to the paper, then, when we'd copied the letters out in our best hand-writing, we slipped them into a post box in the village at the week-end instead of the school box, in case they were opened by accident and the scheme exposed.

'That's that,' Frank said. 'The deed's done. All we do now is wait.'

We could hardly contain ourselves, but for a fortnight nothing happened and Frank's face grew longer. 'They don't want us,' he said.

But the very next day there were two buff envelopes for us, and we slipped out to the playing fields to read them where no one could see us, sitting on the grass behind the cricket pavilion to open them.

'They'll think we're spies receiving missives if they spot us,' Frank grinned as we began to tear open the envelopes.

I felt my heart thump as I saw the heading, 'War Office, Whitehall…'

Frank, who'd been quicker than I had, gave a yelp of excitement. 'They want to see us!' he yelled, leaping at me and hugging me. 'They haven't turned us down, after all!'

I grinned at him and flourished my letter. 'He even has the honour to be my obedient servant,' I said. 'That must mean they're keen.'

—

When I thought about it later I could never quite make out why I'd chosen the Flying Corps. Nobody in the family had ever shown any interest in flying before and Geoffrey only seemed keen because it was clean and got him out of the trenches. I'd had two uncles in the Navy and my father had served with a brother and old Widdows in the Yeomanry in South Africa, but we certainly weren't an aeronautical – or even a very practical – family. My father wrote history for a living and was always occupied with books and research. But like everyone else my age, I'd been fascinated enough to read of the doings of Cody, Blériot, De Havilland and a few more, and had searched magazines for pictures of their machines – exciting but awkward-looking contrivances which seemed all struts, wires and white linen. I'd never quite believed what I'd read about them, though, until I'd seen the one that had turned up outside Norwich three years before, which I'd gone to see with Edith. It was a Beatty-Wright, and it had two propellers driven by bicycle chains from a little engine that sounded like a lawnmower going at full speed. I expect the pilot chose East Anglia because there always seemed to be a strong wind blowing there which would help him to get off the ground and because it was flat enough to come down anywhere in safety if his motor failed. He had never risen more than forty feet off the ground, but he'd *flown*! His machine had lifted him into the air!

In those days we were still sceptical about flying until we saw it before our eyes. We weren't far from the time when they'd measured aeroplanes' power by anchoring them with butcher's spring balances, and they'd taken off on trolleys from rails and landed on skids. It had still been the practice to launch them from the tops of hills so that there was plenty of space beneath for them to float down again. But this machine we saw not only floated downwards in the conventional manner, but actually, first flew upwards, too, under its own power – without the aid of catapults, rails or trolleys, climbing above the trees and circling the field.

From that day on, however, I doubt if I'd ever thought about aeroplanes again and certainly never as a means of going to war. Even now I considered them only because they offered an opportunity to get into uniform a year early and away from the increasingly boring discipline of school.

We sneaked to London the first week-end we could and, hurrying across St James's Park, entered the War Office nervously to find our way up a series of vast staircases and along a dozen different corridors. We were stopped at the end of every one and interrogated by a messenger, as though he thought we'd come to steal military secrets. To our surprise, outside the office to which we'd been directed there was a queue of other young men, some already in uniform.

'Wonder what these chaps want,' Frank said.

I felt vaguely depressed. 'I think *they're* trying to get in the Flying Corps, too.'

Frank's face fell. 'Oh, Lor', no,' he said. 'I hope they've got room for us all.'

He was silent for a moment, then he turned to a young man standing in front of him, in the uniform of a second lieutenant in some Yorkshire regiment.

'What are you waiting for?' he asked.

'To join the Flying Corps,' he was told.

'I hope you're lucky,' Frank said, and the young man in uniform turned to face him.

'What do you mean?' he demanded.

'I've heard they've already got all they want,' Frank said gaily.

The young man stared at him suspiciously and the man next to him, catching what was being said, turned to listen.

'Who told you?' he asked.

'Chap I know,' Frank replied without batting an eyelid. 'He's flying in France. Ever heard of him? The Mad Major?'

Everybody had heard of the Mad Major, though no one ever knew his name. I think he was a fictitious character invented by some newspaper reporter short of copy, but everybody had come to believe he existed – even the soldiers in the front line, who claimed that every machine manoeuvring wildly above their heads was piloted by the fictitious and crazy major.

The young man in uniform nodded. 'Yes,' he said warily. 'I've heard of him.'

'My cousin,' Frank said proudly.

The young man in uniform turned and stared at his next-door neighbour and a buzz of conversation broke out round us.

'What are *you* waiting for, then?' someone asked.

'Navy,' Frank said. 'This is recruits for the Navy.'

'They said downstairs it was for the Flying Corps.'

'No,' Frank said boldly. 'Navy.'

It was a fine lie, standing firmly on its own sturdy legs. It had one flaw, however.

'In the War Office?'

Frank looked floored for a moment, but he rose to the occasion magnificently. 'They're raising naval brigades,' he said, without turning a hair. 'To fight as troops.'

I was staring at him, open-mouthed with admiration, and was just beginning to think he might actually get away with it, and drive everyone away, when the door in front of us opened and a sergeant with a wound stripe and *R.F.C.* plainly marked on his shoulder straps appeared.

'Who's next for flying training?' he demanded.

From then on we were studied by the rest of the queue with hostile suspicion and we were glad when we eventually made it, one after the other, into the office beyond the door. There was an elderly staff captain in there sitting behind a desk. He was bald and smiling and surprisingly helpful.

He took the name of the school and wrote it on a pad in front of him.

'How old are you?' he asked.

'Nearly eighteen, sir,' I said. It was a whopping lie because I was only just seventeen, but I thought if Frank could stretch a point or two, then so could I.

The officer nodded, obviously satisfied, and went on to the next question.

'Play any games?'

I said I did and told him which, but not that I was never particularly good at them.

'Ride a horse?'

I'd ridden horses on the Widdowses' farm, but they'd never been hunters or hacks or anything glamorous. Just a couple of old mares Edith's father kept for rounding up cattle.

'Oh, yes, sir,' I said. 'Often.'

He smiled at me. 'You're still a bit young,' he pointed out.

My heart fell. 'I'm very keen, sir,' I said earnestly.

'Hm.' He seemed to be considering me and I was mentally praying that my face fitted. Then, without saying anything else, he began to write again. I had just begun to decide gloomily that he was setting down all the reasons for rejecting me, so that I could see them in black and white, when he looked up and handed me a note.

'Better take this and show it to the O.C. at Brooklands,' he said. 'He'll tell you what to do.'

I stared at him. 'Am I in, sir?' I asked.

He smiled 'Not yet. There's a long way to go before that. Medicals and a few other things. But I think you're the type. We'll take a chance on you.'

Chapter 2

Shoreham in those days was just a small place on the Brighton-Southampton coast road with a harbour for a coal-and-timber trade at the mouth of the Adur, and a few new bungalows beginning to spring up along the shore to the west. When we arrived by train from Brighton it was already dark and there was a damp salty breeze blowing off the sea.

'Looks like the back end of nowhere,' Frank said, staring round him into the shadows.

He was still with me. We'd both got in and we'd both romped through the medical examination, though some of the questions they'd asked us had puzzled us a bit.

'He seemed damned worried about my teeth,' Frank said indignantly after we'd capered round each other for a while in celebration. 'He seemed to think I wanted to bite the Germans, not shoot 'em.'

We'd been elated with our success, nevertheless. So much so, in fact, that the idea of going back to school had never even crossed our minds. We'd spent the last of our money standing at a bar considering ourselves tremendously adult with a drink in our fists, and had a slap-up meal at what we'd thought was a high-class restaurant but was actually nothing of the kind. Then we'd sent a telegram to the housemaster before setting off home. Mother was shocked when she learned what I'd done. My father took a more realistic view.

'They'll call him up before long anyway,' he said, emerging from the study with an armful of books. 'They're talking about conscription already. And what he's going in for is at least clean and decent.'

The newspapers were still full of the first German gas attacks at Ypres and the Yser Canal, and the horror of this new form of warfare, coming on top of the stale stagnation of the trenches, had sickened people. My mother withdrew her objections almost immediately, realising that at least you couldn't be gassed in the air and feeling that perhaps they wouldn't call on me just yet.

The interview turned out to be quite different from what I'd expected, in fact. I was waiting to be scolded, wept over, perhaps even congratulated. But Geoffrey had turned up from France earlier in the day, on the first leg of his transfer to the R.F.C., and somehow my own news was lost in the relief my mother was feeling that he was out of the trenches and about to enter a branch of the Service that gave him a better chance of surviving. I felt hurt that he'd stolen my big moment and brooded about it a little, and in the evening did what I'd always done in the past when I'd felt the world's weight against me: I went across to the farm to confide in Edith.

Jane met me at the door. She gave me a queer look.

'What do you want?' she said.

'To see Edith.'

Her face split in a knowing smile. 'In the drawing-room,' she said.

I went through the hall – I knew the house as well as I knew my own home – and found Edith sitting at the piano, playing softly to herself. It was something of Chopin's that was quiet and sad, and she was a good enough pianist to make it sound tremendously impressive. She'd done her hair in a grown-up way on top of her head and I'd never seen her look quite so pretty before. It took my breath away.

She was looking at the music, her face expressionless, and I stared at her from the doorway, unseen for a moment, before I spoke.

'Hello, Edith,' I said.

She looked up, her large dark eyes bewildered, and stopped playing at once.

'Martin? What are you doing at home? Term isn't over, is it?'

'No.' I was suddenly shy and dry-mouthed in front of her.

'What then? An epidemic of measles?'

'No,' I blurted out. 'I've left.'

'Left!'

'Walked out. Had enough.'

I moved nearer to the piano and almost at once saw Geoffrey sitting on the arm of a chair at the other side of it, smiling at me in an enigmatic way that was the very essence of big-brotherdom. We stared at each other for a moment, then Geoffrey grinned. Before he could say anything, Edith interrupted so that he couldn't torment me, and I was grateful that she had.

'What are you going to do, then?' she asked, sitting with her hands in her lap, as calm and quiet as if my arrival were a very normal thing.

I was faintly annoyed to find Geoffrey there and very conscious of being the youngest of the three of us. 'They've accepted me for the Flying Corps,' I said. 'Thought I'd just come over and give you the news.'

Edith smiled, a curiously knowing grown-up smile that left me way behind her, still a schoolboy.

'It seems to be infectious,' she said softly. 'Jane had a telegram from Frank' – My word, I thought, he'd been quick – 'and Geoffrey came to do the same thing here – in person.'

I wondered bitterly why it was that Geoffrey always seemed better even at this sort of thing than I was. He'd obviously thought of it first and, judging by the fragile moment I'd broken with my entry, was making a better job of it.

'Oh,' I said, wondering what you had to do to get that look I'd seen in Edith's eyes when I'd first arrived. 'Well, you'll know all about what happens, then.'

Edith smiled again – a kind yet somehow condescending smile. 'Yes,' she said. 'Geoffrey was telling me.'

Geoffrey leaned across the piano. 'What have they taken you on as, son?' he teased. 'Coat-holder for the pilots while they're flying?'

Edith turned on him, indignant and laughing at the same time. 'Geoffrey!'

I knew he was only tormenting me as big brothers had always tormented their juniors from time immemorial, but somehow just then it rankled.

'I'll fly rings round you when I get going,' I said. 'You see.'

I didn't stay long. No one encouraged me to and I felt – for the first time in my life – strangely out of touch with Edith. As I crossed the hall, past the baskets of eggs which Mrs Widdows had put out for the next day's market, Jane swung the door open for me and bowed.

'Oh, shut up!' I snapped.

She straightened up, sweeping her plaits away from her face with a practised jerk of her head. 'I didn't say anything,' she said.

'No, but you were going to!'

For the first time in her life she looked hurt and not ready to give as good as she got.

'No, I wasn't,' she said. 'I was going to say I'd heard you'd joined up.'

'From Frank.'

'Why not?'

'Oh, nothing,' I said. 'It's just that everybody seems a bit quicker off the mark today than I am.'

–

I'd expected the Flying Corps to send for me at once because I'd felt I was already experienced enough to start work. When they'd sent us to Brooklands we'd each been given a short flight in a Longhorn, so-called because of the curving outriggers that held the elevator in front of the pilot. It was an aerial joke, really, and looked like a fully rigged ship with its cat's cradle construction of struts, spars, piano wire and fabric. But it was used a lot for instructional purposes because it flew no faster than sixty miles an hour and if it crashed it simply subsided around you and deposited you gently on the ground surrounded by splintered wood and torn fabric.

It looked roughly like a boy's box kite with additions at front and back, and though it was known by the name of its designer, Maurice Farman, it was always called a Longhorn or, by less respectful people, a 'mechanical cow'. A modern design from the same firm without the curving outriggers was inevitably known as the Shorthorn.

I had struggled with difficulty through the maze of wires to a seat in a thing shaped like a hip bath. The controls looked like a pair of handlebars and the pilot watched my stare of bewilderment as I put my cap on backwards and pulled it well down over my ears. I was trying to work out where all the wires went and what they were all for. He grinned. 'We check by letting a linnet loose inside,' he said. 'If it gets out, there's a wire not connected.'

I learned later that it was an old joke that always raised a laugh, but I was far too nervous to give it my full attention and only smiled politely.

Someone started the seventy-horse Renault motor and as it buzzed away merrily behind I looked down and saw the draught from the propeller stirring the grass. We scuttled across the ground at what seemed a shattering speed, with everything creaking and twanging and rattling around us, and before I'd known what was happening we were in the air. We were even four hundred feet high and the houses looked like boxes. I hadn't been able to believe it.

Except for the knowledge that school was behind us for good, that had been the high point so far, but from that very moment all the ideas I'd ever had of becoming an architect had all gone by the board. There was only one thing I wanted to do now – fly.

But that period of elated anticipation soon passed and we couldn't understand why we weren't sent for. Frank was as bored with doing nothing as I was, and, for lack of anything better to do, came to Norfolk to stay with us.

'They've forgotten us,' he bleated. 'Someone ought to tell 'em they can't possibly win the war without Griffiths. It's a good job there are plenty of girls in Leicester or I might be tempted to join the gravel-crushers in the infantry.'

Despite his professed disappointment, however, I noticed that it didn't stop him getting Jane on one side in the drawing-room and showing her a few new steps he'd picked up at tea dances he'd been to while he'd been waiting. He obviously hadn't been wasting his time and, even while the air was loud with 'Quick-quick-slow – pause – glide', as they practised to the gramophone, he was receiving almost a letter a day from the Midlands, all of them in round feminine hands and all with different post-marks. Since I'd also once caught him kissing Jane in the kitchen when they were supposed to be preparing tea, I felt he was asking too much – and said so.

'It's something you learn,' he grinned. 'It comes from being good-looking and having personality.'

Despite the fact that several months had elapsed since August 1914, when the war had started, no one seemed to have got really organised yet, and, with Frank back in Leicester, the time seemed to drag on for ever. To keep out of my mother's way, I got a job at the Widdowses' farm helping with the spring work.

Because their younger labourers had all been in the Yeomanry and had disappeared into the Army, everyone was doing what they could to help, and I saw a lot of Edith. She'd grown into a surpris-ingly attractive girl, her face suddenly glowing with happiness and *joie de vivre,* and I was unexpectedly shy with her. I'd gone to fairs with her in the past and climbed trees with her. But now she was poised and good-looking enough to take my breath away, and I took to following her about the place, finding jobs that would enable me to be near her.

'You'll have learned enough about farming by the time you're sent for,' she teased me, 'to become a farmer.'

She was always busy in the kitchen, preparing meals for the older labourers who came in at midday, or packing loaves and cheese and tea and taking it out to the fields in the trap. Sometimes I drove her, delighted to be alongside her.

'Ever thought of being a farmer, Martin?' she asked. 'Father says he'd take you on as an apprentice.'

I couldn't think of anything pleasanter. 'Might,' I said. 'When the war's over. How about you?' I went on, greatly daring: 'Ever thought of being a farmer's wife?'

'Not really,' she said.

'What then?' I was prepared to change my mind about my future at the drop of a hat.

'I don't know,' she said. 'It depends.'

'What on?'

'Various things,' she said mysteriously.

I was a little beyond my depth with her. Despite her happiness and the glow in her eyes, she was suddenly somehow unapproachable in a way I couldn't put my finger on. I often found her in the drawing-room playing the piano alone, her eyes dreamy, her fingers wandering over the keys, and sometimes she didn't even see me as I entered and sat down behind her to listen, not understanding a note but prepared to accept the fact to be near her. I never told her what I was feeling, however, because I never had the courage, but I felt she must surely know. She'd known everything about me since we'd been small children and I felt she couldn't possibly fail to understand now.

Jane took a different view. 'You're wasting your time,' she said bluntly.

I stared at her angrily. Jane and I had spent all our lives disagreeing with each other – even sometimes swinging our fists when we were younger. There'd never been any kind of rapport between us because she was as brisk and forthright as Edith was quiet, and she always seemed to know my business better than I did myself.

'Wasting my time doing what?' I demanded. I was blushing furiously as I spoke, because my feeling for Edith was such a private and important one it never crossed my mind that anyone else had an inkling of what I was going through.

Jane stared at me and became maddeningly offhand. 'Oh, nothing,' she said, and I was thankful when she disappeared to school again.

The days dragged on and from time to time I received anxious letters from Frank, wondering if our papers had been lost, and there was even one horrifying period when they pushed up the age of entry to eighteen and we thought they'd throw us out again. The summer drifted in while we grew more and more impatient to get to work, then – at last – we were ordered to report to Brooklands, and were finally in uniform as cadets. We wore double-breasted tunics which were known irreverently as 'maternity jackets' and very smart side hats which always fell off when we bent down.

'Good Lor',' Frank said, staring at himself for the first time in a mirror. 'I look like Abdul the Damned's head waiter.'

'Never mind,' I encouraged. 'We're in.'

He turned and grinned. Actually Frank was a remarkably handsome young man, which was probably why he got so many girls, and he looked very good in uniform.

'That's right,' he said. 'Think we ought to send a telegram to General Haig to say that he can now get on with the war – Griffiths has arrived at last.'

Puttees were the thing that baffled us most.

'If I tie them loosely,' Frank said in bewilderment, 'they fall down. But if I tie them any tighter they stop the circulation.'

We walked out of camp the first night, conscious of an awful feeling of insecurity, and disappeared into the first field we came to, to check that they were safe.

Frank's were in danger of uncurling round his ankles, so I worked on them for him, pulling them tightly so they couldn't slip. When he straightened up, his expression was agonised and when he tried to walk he moved like a toy soldier.

'You ass,' he said. 'You've not allowed any overhang in my trousers. I can't bend my knees.'

–

Because Geoffrey had also just started his training at Shoreham we'd very daringly put in a request for a transfer there from Brooklands and, rather to our surprise, we'd got it. Now, standing on the station with the smell of the sea in our nostrils, I was beginning to wonder if I wouldn't have been wiser to stay where I was. Geoffrey had always been cleverer than I was, better at sports and books, and more of a favourite with my parents because he always showed more sense than I ever seemed to manage. In my heart of hearts I was more than a little afraid of comparison.

He had always intended to read history like my father, but he'd found it difficult to decide against art school because, like my mother, he was a gifted painter, too. The decision for me to become an architect had been a much simpler business. As we'd turned down all the things for which I *wasn't* fitted, we'd remembered that I could also draw a little and was fairly good at maths and had come reluctantly to the conclusion that architecture was the only thing left.

I hadn't even the advantage of Geoffrey's good looks. I looked like my father, dark and heavy-browed, and, even then, somewhere along the line I'd lost the grace that all the other Falconers seemed to have. I was always a little resentful about Geoffrey's easy success. He seemed to have just too many gifts.

As we climbed into the Crossley tender outside the station, I supposed that Geoffrey, with his slender hands, would even be a better pilot than I was. My hands always seemed to be in the way, and about the only thing I could do better than he could was shoot duck. It wasn't much to boast about, really, and Geoffrey even made a joke about that.

'It's the black destruction in your soul,' he'd once told me when he'd missed and I hadn't.

'It's moving with the gun,' I'd replied, self-satisfied because I had the knack and he hadn't. 'Swinging with it, instead of snatching at it, so that the shot arrives at the same spot as the duck.'

'I'd rather paint a duck than shoot it,' he'd said, and it had made me feel small.

So would *I* rather have painted a duck, I'd thought, except that I couldn't paint.

The Crossley deposited us outside the mess, which was a bungalow near the sea. There were cheese and biscuits waiting for us and I was just beginning to feel at home when Geoffrey appeared.

The aerodrome was a mile away from the mess and he arrived with two or three others in the Crossley which had gone to fetch them after picking up Frank and myself. He was still wearing his regimental uniform, and it made him look as handsome as the devil. The R.F.C. maternity tunic was never designed to make a man look smart with its wide front and high collar.

'Well, if it isn't my little brother!' he said, his face splitting in a great beam of pleasure.

I was delighted to see him, of course, as I always was, despite the fact that I envied him so much, but I felt it was a pity he'd had to spoil our meeting with that touch of condescension. Then I decided that if we were going to live together, fly together, perhaps even fight together, I'd got to get over my envy and I knew that the condescension in his tones had never been intentional and was just his usual big brother's chaffing.

By this time, he and Frank were slapping backs and hugging each other.

'I hardly recognised you,' Geoffrey was saying. 'They've disguised you as a soldier.'

'It's no disguise,' Frank grinned. 'I *am* one. I'm *the* soldier, in fact, that the Army's been waiting for.'

'I can just see you,' Geoffrey said. 'Bold as brass and winking at the girls. I bet someone pushed you into it.'

'No. Honest. Own free will and accord.'

'You must be as barmy as I was.' Geoffrey turned to me. 'And look at Martin here, arrogant with martial ardour.'

'Not me,' I said. 'I'm not arrogant. I'm much shyer than I look. If the sergeant speaks to me I'll probably faint.'

The preliminary baiting over, we got down to the serious business of finding out something about the place.

'How long have you been here, Geoff?' Frank was asking.

'Three weeks now.'

'How're you getting on?'

Geoffrey shrugged. 'It's harder than it looks,' he said, and I decided that if it were hard for Geoffrey it would be almost impossible for me.

'Oh, Lor'!' Frank looked worried. 'Why?'

Geoffrey shrugged. 'Well, things never seem to be quite right,' he said. 'If the flag's moving, it's too windy for a Longhorn, and if it's still, there's no "lift" in the air. And if the weather's fine, the machines are unserviceable or the instructor's got the willies.' His voice dropped. 'Some of them are chaps from France and a few of them have got the wind-up, I suspect.'

'Honest?' Frank looked shocked.

'True,' Geoffrey said. 'They won't let go the stick properly. I've got one at the moment. He's always finding excuses not to fly and I swear he's controlling the thing when *I'm* supposed to be doing it. I don't seem to learn much.'

'Can't you do anything about him?'

Geoffrey grinned. 'There are ways and means,' he said, and I knew he'd been exercising his charm in the right quarters. 'I've had a word with one of the other instructors and he's going to take me over. Perhaps now I'll start to make a bit of headway.'

–

We were to be taught on a group of ancient and very battered machines, all of which had seen long service and were now on their last legs before being retired. Loose on the controls, patched and scarred, some of them even the rebuilt survivors of crashes, they weren't terribly encouraging to look at, but kept firmly apart was also a single-seater monoplane that the commanding officer flew, which was actually streamlined and was supposed – though no one had proof – to be capable of a tremendous speed. We eyed it warily, half afraid it might bite, and kept well clear of it.

The instructors, all regular officers who'd learned to fly at their own expense before the war, had already actually been shot at in France. Some were even said to have fought in the air against an enemy machine, performing a sort of slow waltz in a clear sky while the observers took pot shots at each other with rifles.

We went to the field early the first morning, fully expecting to fly immediately. But no one seemed to want to teach us anything. We were allowed to watch – though, for the moment, that seemed to be all we *were* allowed to do – and once we actually saw Geoffrey disappear into the air in a Longhorn and vanish towards the horizon over Brighton. As we watched the machine growing smaller, yearning to do the same, we earnestly discussed its progress with two or three other youngsters whom we thought were experts until we discovered they'd only arrived the week before us and knew very little more than we did. They obviously thought *we* were experts, too, and dropped us hurriedly and started to put on airs when they found we were even newer at the game than they were.

'Any chance of a flip, sir?' I asked one of the leather-clad instructors in desperation. We'd been trying for a week to catch someone's eye.

The instructor shook his head. 'No,' he said. 'Shutting down.'

We weren't sure whether he meant the weather was shutting down or the flying school was shutting down and when Geoffrey returned we crowded round him eagerly.

'How high did you get?' I asked.

'Not very high,' he said knowledgeably. 'Machine wasn't pulling well.'

Frank looked at me nervously. It was all very worrying.

–

The apparent indifference to us was the worst. No one seemed interested in us and, in the hope of picking up some crumb of knowledge, we took to wandering among the machines – ancient Farmans and Blériots and once even a BE2c, which only stayed a day and seemed to us, after the Farmans, the very latest thing. It was a wide-winged biplane with a narrow fuselage that left its crew sitting bolt upright and well and truly exposed to the elements. It had a huge perforated exhaust stack in front to pump the exhaust fumes over the top of the upper wing and was said to be actually capable of mounting a machine-gun. By this time I was so entranced by flying I would have sold my soul for a flight in it. It looked so beautiful I felt sick with envy of the man who piloted it.

Most of the information we acquired we picked up in conversation and by listening to the tall stories of those cadets who'd been there a week or two longer than we had, who'd picked them up from those ahead of *them*. If nothing else we learned very quickly the things we mustn't do and talked of them in awed whispers. Stalling and spinning were events that one dodged like the plague, but it seemed that even dodging was more difficult than we'd imagined, because no one really yet knew what caused you to spin, and stalls were a terrifying prospect that occurred whenever you lost flying speed. Since a Longhorn would stall at about thirty-eight miles an hour, and the top speed of the ancient models we had couldn't have been much more than fifty, there didn't seem much elbow room between climbing into the sky and falling to the ground. And we all knew that if you dared to lower your nose to *avoid* losing speed, you were in danger of overheating your engine – which brought about the same result. If you lowered it *too* far, in fact, you went too fast and pulled the machine apart.

'I can see now,' Frank said, 'why there are so many casualties among pilots. They're all worn out with worry.'

We learned you always had to land into wind, and if your engine cut on take-off – as they seemed to with surprising frequency – you picked out the nearest field at once and put your machine straight down, because if you tried to turn back to the aerodrome, the chances were that you'd lose flying speed, stall and crash. What Frank said wasn't far from the truth.

At first we moved among the aeroplanes nervously, peeping into the cockpits when no one was looking, then growing bolder and actually climbing up to stare at the instruments to try to make out what their function was.

'That's to let you know when it's time for lunch,' Frank said, pointing at a dial. 'When it's straight up, the bugle's due to go.'

'And that one?' I pointed at a compass.

He grinned. 'It's a device to direct you to the girls in Brighton.'

Studying the instruments eventually led to sitting in the machines when there was no one about and moving the controls. But very nervously, because we were always subconsciously afraid that by some miracle the machine would suddenly spring to life and take off.

The older cadets, regarding us with fatherly condescension, were more than willing to impart information. Unfortunately, it wasn't always complete.

'Oh, they're easy enough to get going,' I was loftily told by a plump ginger-haired young man with a toothbrush moustache as I watched a Longhorn start up and float into the air. 'You just turn the engine back first to suck petrol into the cylinders, and after that it's easy. All you have to do is get a good grip of the propeller, swing your leg and pull it down.'

'Promptly getting yourself chopped in half,' Frank said, 'as the engine fires.'

The ginger-haired cadet stared at him coldly. Clearly, starting an aeroplane engine wasn't a thing to joke about.

'You move backwards as you do so,' he said. 'So that you're well clear when it fires.'

He obviously considered Frank was far too flippant and concentrated on me, moving to a Caudron standing in front of the sheds to demonstrate. He began to move the propeller backwards and I watched uneasily as I saw it push against the compression.

'Suppose it starts,' I said nervously. 'Won't it jump forward?'

'Not it,' the plump young man said haughtily. 'It's not switched on. Try it.'

It seemed easy enough. I took a firm grip on the propeller and threw all my weight backwards.

–

There was a terrific explosion that took me completely by surprise. It was followed by a roar, and, to my horror, the Caudron jumped the chocks in front of the wheels and leapt at me like a mad animal intent on swallowing me whole.

I saw Frank bolt for safety, his head down between his arms, and I dived wildly for the ground, sprawling on the grass, sick at heart and terrified at what I'd done. The switch *was* on, and I saw the shadow of the wing pass over me as the Caudron rolled forward, then I was up like a jack-in-a-box behind it. Unfortunately, there was a Maurice Farman standing nearby, and with a heart-rending 'scrunch' the Caudron charged it at full throttle, digging its left wing into the right-hand tail-boom of the Farman, while the propeller, turning at twelve hundred revs a minute, began to chew its way through the Farman's interplane struts.

People looked up at the noise and started to run and I leapt about, searching wildly around me for the fool who'd misled me, to stop it or at least tell *me* how to stop it. But he'd vanished, as though a hole in the ground had opened up and swallowed him, and I was still dancing around, yelling for help while the Caudron worked its way through two tail-booms and a wing. By this time, someone had managed to reach the cockpit and the propeller finally stopped as he switched off. The silence seemed enormous.

'What the hell do you think you're up to?' A furious face was thrust into mine. It was Geoffrey's instructor, a tall, burly, tired-looking man who was in a perpetual bad temper. He was known as Ferdinand, because he was said to resemble some vague Balkan potentate who was supposed to be about to come down on the side of the Germans and therefore had a reputation for treachery.

'The switch was on,' I gulped.

His eyebrows danced a jig of rage on his forehead.

'Well, why the hell didn't you switch it off instead of letting them chop each other up, you blasted idiot?'

The air was full of drifting blue castor-oil smoke, and crowds of men – noticeably not the one who'd instructed me – were appearing from all directions, armed with fire extinguishers, axes, and even ladders. As they pulled the machines apart, they were asking each other what had happened, while I tried hard to look completely innocent. Ferdinand shouted a few orders and set them to work, then he suddenly remembered me, and turned to Frank and another cadet.

'You two! Fall in! Escort this man to his room!'

As we marched away, Frank leaned over and spoke out of the side of his mouth.

'Don't worry, Martin,' he said. 'They won't give you more than five years.'

Chapter 3

'What's it like in the condemned cell?' Frank asked.

He seemed to regard the whole incident as a great joke and for most of the time I felt like throwing something at him, because it was no joke for me.

The major in charge of training happened to be away and I was confined for five days to my room, except for meals or exercise, always with Frank in attendance, while the cadet who'd egged me on seemed to have vanished into thin air. When Frank's enquiries on my behalf failed to produce a culprit and a confession I decided he'd deserted or committed suicide and that I'd have to bear the blame alone.

Eventually the major returned and I was ordered to his office. He was a man called Seago who'd been one of the very first pilots to fly to France in 1914 when aeroplanes had been so rare they hadn't even worn national insignia. In the short time I'd been at Shoreham I'd acquired a tremendous respect for him that amounted almost to hero-worship.

He was a tall man, with a beak of a nose and long thin legs which were made to look even thinner by the tight canvas leggings he wore. He was an ex-cavalryman and always wore a choker stock round his long neck, so that as he strolled about the field he looked vaguely like an absent-minded stork. But to people like me, his record of forced landings due to engine failures and brushes with enemy aeroplanes made him as near as you could get to one of the ancient heroes of legend. It was said he'd actually destroyed a German machine and there was also a story that once he'd had to force-land behind the enemy lines, but, repairing a broken fuel pipe, had taken off again over the heads of the Uhlans who were charging forward to capture him. It pained me even to have to suffer his icy contemptuous stare.

'I ought to give you detention,' he said. 'No other cadet would even *think* of swinging a propeller without checking first that the switch was off.'

I felt like saying that, as it happened, one had, or at least had suggested that *I* should, but I held my tongue.

'You've practically destroyed two perfectly good machines,' he went on. 'If you'd been a mechanic

I'd have sent you to detention. As it is, I'm going to confine you to camp and see that you do extra duties for the next fortnight.'

Already utterly devoted to flying after my one brief trip, it seemed to me a savage sentence, though – allowing for the treachery of the ginger-haired cadet – one I felt I absolutely deserved.

Like Frank, Geoffrey seemed to regard the incident as a huge joke.

'Just think,' he pointed out. 'You've destroyed more machines now than Seago.'

'*Our* machines,' I growled.

'Perhaps the Kaiser'll offer you a job,' he grinned. 'With *his* lot.'

I didn't take very kindly to his teasing. I felt too much like a criminal, and there were one or two of the other cadets – self-satisfied young men well imbued with the honour of their calling and rather smug because *their* errors had never been found out – who quite definitely did look on me as a criminal. They felt I'd spoiled their chances of flying, and it was certainly true that I'd drastically reduced the number of available aircraft, which was never many. At the same time, I felt they had no cause for complaint, as the only one who was suffering at all seemed to be me.

As it happened, I didn't fall behind the others because instruction for our group was still confined to lectures – on navigation, aerodynamics and meteorology. There was still no flying and by staying up to the early hours, sitting perched and chilled on a stool in the bath-house after lights out while everyone else was asleep, I was able to write up my notes by the beam of a torch and keep abreast.

During the whole fortnight I was under punishment I brooded over the injustice I'd suffered and searched for the know-all who'd got me into trouble. He'd been a pompous young man and I was itching to get my hands on him, and I watched for him in the dining-hall and was on the look-out whenever I visited the guardroom. But he was lying low and I failed to find him until a week after the shackles were removed and I was a free man again. He'd panicked, I learned later, and, realising that I might accuse him, had established an alibi by bolting at once to the sick quarters in the confusion of the crash and claiming to be suffering from a stomach infection. When Frank, who'd questioned every single cadet on the field on his whereabouts at the time of the disaster, had approached him he'd been able to say he'd not even been there and had offered evidence to back up his statement.

I bumped into him quite by accident as I turned the corner of the hangars with Frank. I was just beginning to feel once more a normal civilised member of society, and as we almost collided all the injustice of my punishment welled up in me. I'd happily have served my sentence if he'd confessed and joined me, and the fact that he'd dodged his share of responsibility had rankled from the word go.

'You!' I said.

He'd stopped dead, his face pale, and I stared at him furiously.

'I just did a fortnight's punishment because of you, you dirty tyke,' I said.

He was an unlikable young man who later dropped out of the course rather abruptly, and, unable to back away from me, he threw the accusation back at me at once, his ginger eyelashes blinking rapidly.

'It was your own fault,' he said. 'I warned you.'

'You did nothing of the sort!'

'I told you the switch was on.'

'Then why the hell did you bolt when the engine started?'

He tried to bluster it out. 'You chaps never learn,' he said. 'I expect you probably even did it deliberately because you were afraid of having to fly the thing.'

It was just too much. I don't remember hitting him but the next thing I realised he was lying on his back, holding his nose, while his eyes looped the loop in their sockets and I stood over him, red-faced and furious, inviting him to get up so I could have the pleasure of knocking him down again. He didn't seem anxious to respond to the invitation and stayed where he was, then I realised that Frank, who was standing just behind me, was wearing a horrified expression. I couldn't think why at first, because punching someone in the nose for what he'd done to me didn't seem anything very terrible. Then, as my gaze followed Frank's, I realised why he looked so sick. Ferdinand, the instructor, was standing by the corner of the hangar, his long nose thrust out, his eyes narrow.

'What the devil's going on here?' he demanded.

We all slammed to attention at once, my stomach sinking to my boots.

'Nothing, sir,' I said.

'Were you fighting?'

'Oh, no, sir! An accident, that's all.'

He gave a low sarcastic laugh. 'I suppose he fell against your fist, eh? Well, we'll see about that. Report to the guardroom at once.'

The following day I was in front of Seago again, charged this time with conduct prejudicial to good discipline or something else equally vague. Ferdinand gave his evidence briskly and Seago fixed me with a steely stare.

'You've hardly finished your punishment for the last offence,' he snapped. 'And you know that brawling where there are aircraft could be dangerous, both to yourself or to the crew of a machine.' He studied me for a while, frowning, then he seemed abruptly to lose interest. 'You'd better do another fortnight,' he said. 'And this time I warn you there won't be another chance. Any more trouble and you've failed.'

Another fortnight of permanent duty when I'd just been congratulating myself that I'd finished was depressing, but at least I'd had the satisfaction of getting a little of my own back on the man who'd first caused it all. It almost seemed worth it.

'I shouldn't try it again, though,' Frank advised cheerfully, 'or you'll find yourself out on your neck.'

–

As it happened, once again I was fortunate. Although our group were due to fly at last, the punishment this time coincided with a fortnight of filthy weather that virtually ended all activity, and when my punishment was finished I found I still hadn't dropped behind.

Training was still very much a hit-or-miss affair because no one had written any training manuals at that time and there was remarkably little standardis-ation. A lot depended on the instructor you'd been allotted and I certainly didn't think much of mine because he turned out to be the one Geoffrey had got rid of – my old friend, Ferdinand. My fondness for him was equalled only by his fondness for me.

'You, eh?' he said when I appeared. 'Well, you'd better do jolly well or I shall fail you. I shall be *looking for faults* because it strikes me you're just the type we can best do without.'

His very attitude towards me put me on edge at once and made me nervous with my flying, and he was always brusque, gruff and rude, no matter how hard I tried or how polite and respectful I tried to be. He never made sure I'd grasped or even heard what he was telling me, and I soon began to feel I was dropping rapidly behind. Geoffrey had long since gone solo and was flying circuits of the field on his own now, and even Frank seemed to be way ahead of me. I decided that it was just the old story of everyone else being better at it than I was.

'It's my belief,' Frank said, listening to my woes, 'that some of these instructors – and Ferdinand's one – are so relieved to be back in England they've no intention of risking their necks with us.'

Certainly Ferdinand didn't show much interest except to be unpleasant, and I picked up most of my knowledge by shyly trying to talk to some of the cadets who'd been noticed already, wistfully hoping that some instructor with a better temper would eventually hear me asking questions.

By this time I'd come to the conclusion that flying was a little like tightrope walking. It seemed you either crashed the machine you were flying by going too fast and tearing the wings off or by going too slow and stalling. Whichever way it went, the chances were that you'd break your neck.

There were a few lectures, but the weather was still so indifferent there wasn't a great deal of flying – particularly with Ferdinand. As Geoffrey had pointed out, when the flag stirred on its pole, he said it was 'too gusty' and when it didn't he claimed there was no 'lift' in the air. With Ferdinand the margin between possible and impossible was mysteriously narrow.

Occasionally someone went solo, so I had to accept there was some organisation somewhere, and I used to wait outside the hangar, my heart in my mouth, staring with awe at successful pupils or smiling and making clever remarks if they failed by the simple process of breaking something as they landed. Fortunately, no one broke his neck, though there were plenty of minor accidents and one very spectacular one when one aeroplane landed on top of another. The two machines rolled themselves into a tight knot of wood, wire and canvas, but, as we tore across the field ready to drag the stiffening corpses from the shambles, a furious instructor rose from the debris and proceeded to berate at the top of his voice the shamefaced cadet who'd been guilty of not looking where he was going. Neither of them was hurt.

I had one preliminary flight in the Longhorn, which was nothing more than a gentle float round the field at about five hundred feet, and straight down again, and then nothing else for a fortnight. Then suddenly Ferdinand seemed to wake up to the fact that I existed.

Instruction still remained so casual, however, I remained entirely in the dark about the function of the various parts of the machine or even about what some of the instruments were supposed to tell me. The one thing that seemed to be important was to be ready quickly and in the high passenger's seat without keeping him waiting. After several flights, though, he actually allowed me to grip the handlebar controls. They looked a little like a pair of spectacles and between working these and shoving at the rudder pedals with my feet, flying seemed to be a cross between riding a bicycle and pumping the organ in the church at Fynling.

Ferdinand always seemed to me to be edgy and nervous and was far too impatient to be an instructor. He would shut off the engine from time to time to shout to me what he was doing, but he was also in the habit of swearing a lot and went in for a great deal of angry arm-waving on the ground so that I didn't learn much from him. Like Geoffrey I soon became convinced that even when he told me to take over he still kept his hands on the controls and manoeuvred the Longhorn himself.

I was so fed up with learning nothing, I decided to test him.

When he next told me to try a few take-offs and landings I simply used the throttle and just touched the controls with my finger-tips, and sure enough they moved of their own volition as soon as we reached flying speed and the machine lifted into the air. I grinned, fascinated, and took my hands away entirely to leave it to Ferdinand.

The machine circled the field several times, banking neatly, and settling into position for its final approaches and landings, the controls still moving without any help from me. As we turned for our final glide-in and I cut the engines, the nose went down once more on its own and we floated gently to the grass.

I was still enjoying the joke as we taxied up to the hangar and was looking forward to telling Frank, but as we stopped, Ferdinand began to climb out without switching the engine off.

'Did that jolly well,' he said gruffly. 'Better than I thought you'd be. Take her up now and go solo.'

I gaped at him. The struts and wires still had remarkably little meaning for me, and there was still a vast amount of the unknown about flying. As for actually taking the Longhorn up without help...

'I've only had an hour and a half's instruction,' I offered nervously.

Inevitably, he became angry at once. His long nose twitched and he began to shout. 'I'm the one who decides whether you're good enough or not,' he yelled. 'Take her up!'

I could see myself getting up in the air and flying round for ever because I didn't know how to get down, and his anger started my own quick temper.

'I've never handled her properly yet!' I snorted.

He glared. 'You just took her off and landed her – several times.'

My rage exploded. 'I never touched the damned thing!' I shouted, as angry as he was now. 'You did the lot – on your own!'

His temper flared up furiously. 'Take her up!' he roared. 'Or are you scared?'

I saw the waiting mechanics eyeing each other, because I was yelling as wildly as Ferdinand now. 'Yes!' I screamed. 'And so would you be if you'd never been told a damn' thing that's any good. You're asking me to break my neck doing something you've never shown me how to do or given me a chance to do!'

Ferdinand almost burst with rage. Inevitably, I found myself bound for Seago's office once more.

-

Sitting behind his desk, Seago peered at Ferdinand over his beak of a nose while he said his piece, then he waved him out of the room and sat back in his chair to stare at me, his pale blue eyes icy.

'I didn't expect to see you here again, Falconer,' he said quietly.

'No, sir,' I said wretchedly. 'Neither did I.'

'I'd hoped you'd make as much progress as your brother.'

Here it came – the inevitable comparison with Geoffrey.

'So did I, sir,' I muttered.

Seago was silent for a moment. 'You're even having trouble with your flying now.'

'Yes, sir,' I agreed. 'I am a bit.'

'In fact, if I hear things correctly, you're *refusing* to fly.'

'I did refuse, sir, yes, but…'

'That's a very serious thing to do. When people refuse to fly we have to assume that they're not at one with us and are best posted to the Army.'

'Sir…'

He signed me to silence. 'I've had to punish you twice before,' he told me. 'You were responsible for fighting with another cadet on the tarmac and for the loss of two aircraft due to carelessness.'

'Yes, sir. That was my fault entirely.'

For a moment he stared at me in silence. 'As a matter of fact,' he said, 'I've heard since – and it doesn't matter how – that it wasn't; that you were, in fact, informed by another cadet – the cadet you assaulted, curiously – that the switch was off. You took your punishment without complaining.'

'I should have looked myself, sir.'

He gave a little frown. 'Yes, you should,' he agreed. 'However, that's over and done with. Why are you refusing to fly? You seem to have plenty of spirit.'

I took a deep breath. It didn't seem worth while trying to avoid incriminating other people. Seago appeared to have means of finding out, anyway. And I was desperately keen to fly. I was determined that the stupidity of one man wasn't going to stop me.

'Because I've never been taught anything, sir,' I said.

Seago's eyes fell to my records on his desk. 'According to your log-book, you've flown about three hours.'

'Not on my own, sir! I've never once had proper control of the aircraft.'

For a moment he stared at his finger-tips which he'd placed together in the form of a steeple, then he looked up at me and smiled. It was a charming smile, and all the more so because I'd never seen it before.

'Meet me at the hangars tomorrow morning,' he said. 'I'll see what you can do.'

That night Frank came in with the news that Ferdinand had been taken off flying.

'He was months in France, it seems,' he said. 'And a series of bad crashes and narrow escapes broke his nerve so that he was terrified by instructing dummies like you and me.'

'How do you know?' I asked. 'Did *he* tell you?'

'No. I got it from one of the chaps, who got it from the sergeant in the orderly room.'

'That's a wonderful source,' I pointed out sarcastically. 'Where did the sergeant get it?'

He threw his helmet at me furiously. 'Well, he's been given a different job now, anyway,' he said loudly. 'He's not on orders for instructing tomorrow. Go and have a look for yourself. It's to give him a chance to recover properly.'

As it happened, what Frank had said turned out to be true, because *I* made a point of asking a few people who might know. I didn't regard it as a victory, however, because, despite his ill-temper, it had been Ferdinand, of all people, who'd found out who'd been responsible for the disaster to the Caudron and the Farman. It was Geoffrey who gave me the information.

'So perhaps you'll think a little more kindly of him now,' he said, curiously concerned for Ferdinand.

'He didn't teach me to fly,' I said. 'He was afraid.'

Geoffrey laid a hand on my shoulder. 'I hope you'll remember what you've just said,' he remarked, 'when you've been to France and in action as long as he was.'

I saw what he meant and I felt no joy at Ferdinand's disappearance because I suddenly began to realise how much strain he'd been through and felt desperately sorry for him.

I was at the hangar the following morning – far too early, because I was terrified of being late. I seemed to hang about for hours, worried sick I'd got Seago's instructions wrong and that I'd be in trouble again for not paying attention, then he finally appeared, sauntering across the field on his long thin legs, carrying a leather coat and helmet, his nose in the air as though he were trying to catch the scent of the flowers that studded the hedgerows.

'Sorry,' he apologised. 'Held up. Climb in.'

I dragged on my helmet and clambered through the wires of the Longhorn to my seat and we took off. He went through the principles and rules of take-off, climb, straight and level flight, gentle turns, gliding with the engine off, and landing, always patient, clear and concise.

'Don't let her nose go down below the angle of glide and speed I showed you,' he said as he climbed out after landing.

'No, sir,' I said stoutly. 'I won't.'

'Right' – he seemed to have lost interest in me – 'away you go!'

I stared at him. Away I went?

My stomach felt as empty as a drum. I wasn't ready for this. I felt I hardly knew a thing and what I'd learned this unexpected crisis had caused me to forget. The Longhorn suddenly seemed an absolute mystery to me and for a moment I felt that even Seago, whom I now revered more than ever, had betrayed me. He was already walking away into the hangar, not even looking back, and I felt hurt that this man whom I admired so much couldn't even be bothered to stop and see me kill myself.

Then, gathering my wits and subduing the panic in me, I decided that if he, who had a reputation second to none, was so casual about what I did, he must be fairly sure I could do it. Though I had had so short a period of instruction, other people also went solo after short periods, and the Longhorn, for all its faults, was an uncomplicated grandmotherly old machine which seemed to look after the people who flew it. Although I was momentarily shocked by the responsibility that had been thrust at me, I knew I *could fly* it and realised that Seago's act of turning his back was a deliberate show of indifference to give me confidence.

I saw the mechanics standing nearby. They'd obviously been waiting to wheel the machine back into the hangar when Seago had climbed out.

'Are we finished, sir?' one of them asked.

'No, I'm taking her up.'

They exchanged glances and I felt sure I saw pity in their faces at my youth. Then they became brisk and businesslike. One reached for the ropes of the chocks and the other approached the propeller.

'Switch off?' he said.

'Switch off,' I replied nervously, settling into the front seat of the nacelle and thinking how uncomfortable and exposed it seemed.

'Contact?'

'Contact.'

The mechanic's leg swung, the propeller jerked, and the engine clattered into life. I stared round. The mechanic was grinning at me and I felt sure I discerned a sneer in the gesture.

I swallowed hard, determined to wipe it off his face with a brilliant virtuoso performance, and waved away the chocks. Sitting tensely in the seat, as though I were controlling a monster that might break loose at any moment, and pushing nervously at the rudder pedals as though they were made of fragile china, I fixed my eyes firmly on the forward elevator.

Keeping my eyes stiffly in front, as though they were nailed to their sockets, I was terrified of losing concentration and causing the machine to do one of the awful things I'd heard they did from time to time. Things that no one knew very much about like stalling or, that terror of terrors, spinning. After a while, very cautiously, in case the movement upset the delicate balance of the machine, I slid my gaze to the altimeter. I was exhilarated by what I saw. I was up! Three hundred feet up! And on my own!

On my own? The realisation came to me with a shock. Not only was I up on my own, but I had to get down on my own, too. I'd heard several people say 'Any fool can fly an aeroplane. It's getting it down that matters.' Now I knew what they meant.

A careful slither of my eyes to my wrist watch showed me that I'd been up for four minutes, and I saw that I'd already left Worthing behind me. If I didn't turn soon, I'd be over country I'd never flown over before and be utterly lost. Beyond that, if I wasn't careful, lay Land's End, the Atlantic and oblivion.

I pushed the nose down slightly and moved the handlebars and, wonder of wonders, the machine banked slowly over the sea – just as it should – like the lazy wheel of a seagull. A little pressure of the foot, talking aloud to myself all the time – 'Look out for stalling. Watch for spinning. And don't push the nose down too far because Longhorns are supposed to fall apart at sixty-five miles an hour' – and the river at Shoreham came in sight again and I turned gently once more over the harbour. A careful movement of eyes once more to the speed indicator – not too hurriedly though, because I felt I was sitting on a very uncertain jelly that might slide from under me if I put too much effort into looking – then, to my joy, the aerodrome was in front of me again, and I saw the pupils watching on the tarmac, ready to laugh if I crumpled the machine up in landing or rush to my assistance if I was hurt. Seago was among them, taller and thinner than any of them, head up, watching me carefully, and my heart warmed to him. He hadn't abandoned me, after all.

All I had to do now was get down. Muttering aloud a mixture of prayers, imprecations and all the instructions I'd ever been given, I cut the throttle and held the nose down to keep flying speed, handling the machine as though it were made of meringue. Forty-one miles an hour. Perfect.

I seemed to be doing all right. Nothing had fallen off yet and I could hear a gentle rushing sound around me and a singing from the wires as we floated slowly downwards. The green blur of the field became individual blades of grass and I pulled back on the stick a little. The nose lifted. A glance at the speed indicator showed me I was on the point of stalling.

In alarm, I was just thinking of putting down the nose again when I felt a faint rumbling beneath me and the machine creaked and the wires twanged, and I realised that what I was thinking of doing was impossible. I was down as far as I could go. I was on the ground. I had gone solo.

Seago appeared alongside as I stopped. He seemed to have lost interest in me again.

'Not too painful, was it?' he said lazily.

'Oh, no, sir!' I was ecstatic. 'It was tremendous!'

'Splendid. Taxi her to the shed.'

As I finally switched off and climbed out, Frank galloped across. I was still a little drunk with excitement at the thought that I'd taken off and landed entirely on my own.

'What was it like?' he demanded.

I pretended an indifference I'd never come within a mile of feeling in the air. 'Had to look out for the old spin once or twice,' I said grimly.

His look of awe made my heart leap.

Chapter 4

As it happened, Frank wasn't long after me with his own first solo and we were finally accepted as permanent members of the Flying Corps and granted commissions. We were suddenly no longer schoolboys on probation but, according to the certificates we received, 'trusty and well-beloved' officers in the special reserve.

'Just think,' Frank said, smiling all over his face as he read the carefully printed words, 'we hold the special confidence of "George, by the Grace of God, of the United Kingdom of Great Britain and Ireland, and the British Dominions beyond the Seas, King, Defender of the Faith, Emperor of India, etc." Just think of that.'

'It's quite a thought,' I agreed. 'Wonder if he'd like any help running Buckingham Palace.'

We removed all the shameful badges of cadetship and bought Sam Browne belts we didn't know how to wear, and began to strut a little, putting on the same airs and graces in front of newcomers that we'd once had to endure ourselves.

We fully expected to pass on rapidly to more sophisticated machines than the antiquated Longhorns, but the following week there was a spell of dreadful weather which effectively stopped all training. The rain lashed down in torrents and left the field so much under water all flying had to stop until it dried out. We were furious – until we found ourselves heading for London and thence home for a long week-end leave. Geoffrey, already ahead of us on his course and by this time flying vast distances into the blue as far as Gosport in Caudrons, Avros and BEs, had already gone on leave to celebrate receiving his wings.

We had stared enviously at the modest little badge on his breast which meant so much to us. It wasn't very elaborate or colourful, but it meant that he was now a qualified pilot and was waiting for a posting to France. Our hopes of going with him had diminished as he'd raced away from us, and all we could hope for now was that he could pull a few strings and get us posted to the same squadron.

The train to London was crowded, but Frank was far from put off by the crowded compartment.

'Think your measles are quite better?' he asked me loudly as we dumped our bags on the rack and settled down.

Half a dozen pairs of eyes flicked at once towards us, and I knew what he was up to because he'd done it on other occasions returning from school.

'Just about,' I said. 'How about yours?'

'Hard to say,' he replied off-handedly. 'They say it's always more infectious after the spots have gone.'

There was a hasty emptying of the compartment at the next station and Frank stretched himself across the seat.

'If I could think of something more infectious than measles,' he said happily, 'I bet I could clear a whole train in twenty minutes.'

I hadn't been able to send a warning telegram to say I was coming, but the village grocer at Fynling used his van as a taxi service and I managed to get a lift home in that. My first idea when I arrived was to dash over to the Widdowses' farm and tell Edith about going solo. I'd imagined her enthusiasm and pleasure all the way home, but when I got there she was out. Geoffrey had called for her in the pony and trap to take her to Norwich. I felt deflated and faintly annoyed. Geoffrey always seemed to be ahead of me. I supposed he was telling her about his wings.

Jane watched me, her eyes merry and derisive.

'Tell me instead,' she suggested. 'I'll listen, even if Edith won't.'

I'd never really noticed Jane much before, because she'd been passing through that plaited, long-legged, narrow-hipped state of growing up that was thoroughly uninteresting in girls. But she was a good listener, I had to admit, and I was dying to boast to someone. Curled up in a chair in the kitchen, her eyes shone as I described my passage-of-arms with the plump cadet and my eventual triumph over Ferdinand.

She was awed enough even for me.

'I say, Martin,' she breathed, 'what a nerve!'

'Oh, well' – I put on an act of becoming modesty – 'you have to have a bit of nerve to be a pilot, you know.'

'Is going solo a bit like finding for the first time that you can swim?' She was a good swimmer and the comparison seemed reasonable.

'A bit,' I agreed. 'But much better.'

She shifted restlessly in the chair. 'Tell me some more about it,' she urged. 'What did it feel like?'

I tried to use all the technical terms I knew to make it sound important, but she stopped me dead.

'Not like that, idiot! What did it *feel* like? What did you *think*? Were you *scared*?'

'Not really,' I said. 'I was too busy.'

'I bet you never thought you could, did you?'

'No, I didn't,' I admitted. 'At least not until I got off the ground. But I knew then that if I didn't get down, I certainly couldn't go on flying for ever either. One chap got so scared he flew round till his petrol ran out, and then, because he had no idea what to do for a forced landing, he crashed.'

'Was he killed?'

'No, you bloodthirsty little beast, he wasn't! They chucked him out though. He had to go back to his regiment. He said he preferred being shot at by the Germans, anyway, to floating round in the air.'

Her eyes gleamed. 'What about you? What did you feel when you knew you had to get down?'

I grinned. 'Well, I gritted my teeth and pushed my prow-like jaw forward' – her eyes widened – 'it was do or die, you know. Death or glory. My country needed me. My eyes blazed and I screwed up my courage and grasped my sword – I mean, the controls…'

She flung a book at me. 'You're pulling my leg,' she yelled.

–

That evening I decided to try again to see Edith, but my mother told me she didn't think it would be convenient.

'Why not?' I said. 'She's back. I saw the trap pass the house towards the farm an hour ago.'

'Oh – well' – my mother seemed to be searching for something in her mind – 'well, Geoffrey's staying to help her with her father's accounts.'

'Again?'

She'd obviously forgotten that she'd tried that one before and for a moment was at a loss what to say.

'They can always put them on one side for a bit,' I said. 'Edith'll want to know about me going solo. She always did want to know what I was up to.'

'I think you'd better stay here,' my mother said. 'They'll be busy.'

'They won't mind,' I urged. 'Perhaps Edith'll be glad to have me. Geoff's hopeless at maths.'

My mother stared hard at me. 'I think Geoffrey and Edith will manage very well, Martin,' she said firmly.

I was irritated by her rigid attitude. 'But, Mother, I wanted to have a word with Edith…!'

She pushed me in front of her towards the stairs. 'Not just now,' she said. 'I've got a job for you. I want you to help me move that chestful of Geoffrey's books up to the attic.'

I stared. 'Can't Geoff do it?' I bleated indignantly.

'He's busy.'

'So am I.'

'Not so busy as he is. And he won't be wanting them now because he won't be going to the university until after the war, and they're only in the way.'

I was puzzled. Geoffrey had once told me he'd decided to put shelves up in his bedroom, and arrange the books on them round the gramophone on which he liked to play heavy classical records with a dreamy look in his eyes.

I tried again. 'But Geoff said…'

She gave me a little push. 'Upstairs,' she said sharply, and this time I accepted that there was no arguing with her.

I had intended to tackle Geoffrey about the mystery when he came home, because I'd been doing a lot of thinking during the evening and coming to a lot of unexpected conclusions. Too many people seemed to be in on a secret that didn't include me, and it all seemed to add up to something ominous. But Geoffrey was late and I decided that old Widdows' accounts must be in a pretty rotten state for him and Edith to take half the night sorting them out – if, indeed, that was what they *were* doing.

I determined to have it out with someone and get an answer and when, the following morning, I had to drive my mother to the station to catch the train to Norwich to do some shopping, I decided the time was ripe. I drove the pony home far too fast, and hardly managed to find time to rub her down and turn her into the loose box before I bolted to the Widdows farm as fast as I could go, in case my father appeared with some excuse to stop me. I wasn't very surprised when I found Geoffrey's bicycle propped up outside the door.

I stared at it, frowning. Strong suspicions had been forming in my mind during the night and I couldn't believe that old Widdows' accounts were proving *that* tricky.

Jane let me in. 'Where's Edith?' I demanded.

'Out.'

'Oh!' This wasn't really unexpected, either, but it rather took the wind out of my sails. I'd expected that by arriving early she'd still be occupied about the house and I could have had it out with her.

'Where?' I asked.

'Down by the river.'

I stared at the sunshine outside. 'What's she doing down there?'

'She's with Geoffrey.'

'I don't suppose they're swimming,' I said.

She stared back at me, her eyes wide. 'I don't suppose they are,' she agreed. 'You're not going down there, are you?'

'No,' I said. 'Not this time.'

'Good job. Two's company, three's none.'

'Yes.'

She came nearer, and I noticed her eyes were sympathetic now. 'Has it dawned on you at last?' she asked.

'What?'

'About Edith and Geoffrey.'

'Yes,' I said. 'The penny's dropped.'

'It took long enough,' she said sharply. 'You really were an ass, blundering about on your great flat feet, getting in the way.'

I stared at her, realising that my journey to the farm had been unnecessarily dramatic and had all along been quite pointless. 'I suppose that what I'm thinking – what you're thinking…'

'Of course, you idiot!' Her face was disgusted. 'They've gone all soppy about each other.'

'Seems funny,' I said.

Despite her contempt, she suddenly and bewilderingly switched sides. 'Why?' she demanded. 'What's funny about it?'

'Well, Edith's only just over a year older than me.'

She gave a laugh. 'That makes her eighteen,' she pointed out. 'And she's a jolly sight older than you are in behaviour. All girls are. Even *I* knew what was going on. You've just been stumbling about blind as a bat.'

'Yes, I know.'

She switched sides again, showing her irritation. 'They've been mooning about over each other for ages,' she said. 'It was bad enough when Geoffrey was last on leave. Now it's dreadful.'

I had to accept that it was true. It was obviously true. But I'd always thought Edith was closer to me than Geoffrey. We'd grown up together. I just hadn't been able to absorb the fact that she could fall in love with anyone else – not even my brother.

'I found it hard to believe,' I said. 'That's all.'

'It's nice to know you've started.'

I shrugged. 'Funny,' I said. 'I always thought that if Edith fell for anyone she'd fall for me.' My mind fled back to a scene at the very same river where she was now with Geoffrey. She'd told me solemnly that she'd marry me when she grew up. She'd been nine at the time, but I'd never forgotten it.

'I always thought all along that she'd end up by marrying me,' I said slowly.

'Well' – Jane laughed – 'it looks as though you've got another think coming. She won't be marrying you *now*.' She paused and stared at me mischievously. 'I'll tell you what, though,' she said.

'What?'

'If you'll wait a bit, *I* will.'

–

I walked home slowly across the fields deep in thought and, halfway, sat on a gate to chew a piece of grass and work things out.

I'd known all night, really, about Edith and Geoffrey. Jane had been trying to tell me about it for ages, and I'd been too stupid to see. For all her faults, Jane was always frank and honest and I felt grateful that she'd tried to break it to me gently.

There was still a sense of hurt and betrayal, though, because I hadn't yet got used to the idea and, bewildered, I went home and took out the punt. I didn't take the gun with me because it wasn't the season and I didn't feel like shooting, anyway. I just wanted to be alone. I was terrified that Jane might turn up at the house, ready to jeer at me again, and, surprisingly, nervous of meeting Geoffrey or Edith. Our lives, so tightly bound together up to now, seemed to be beginning to separate. I'd been troubled for some time by Geoffrey's newly acquired attitudes to the war, his cool, faintly cynical approach to my romantic ideals, and with Edith's suddenly apparent maturity and quiet self-assurance. And now, somehow, at the back of my mind, I felt unreasonably that there'd been treachery.

I avoided the family for the rest of the week-end and, back at Shoreham, Frank was the first to notice that something was wrong with me. When I appeared from the field on the first day after returning from leave he was waltzing round the room to the gramophone, with a cushion clutched to his chest.

'What the devil are you doing?' I said, frowning at the din.

'Foxtrot,' he said. 'Tried it?'

'Not me. I get in a knot even doing a waltz. You're making a devil of a row.'

'You need it loud. It's harder than the Bunny Hug and you need to hear the rhythm.' He stared at me, bright-eyed, cheerful and handsome, but mature and wise in the ways of the world. 'You feeling off colour?' he asked.

'No,' I told him. 'I'm all right.'

'You look like a sick cow. You *sure* you're all right?'

'Yes,' I snapped. 'I'm sure.'

'No need to shout!' He stared at me. 'You been falling for a girl?' he said.

I stared at him and he grinned.

'People do,' he said. 'Or so I've noticed.'

'Do I look as if I had?'

'Thought you had that lost look of someone in love. I met a ripping girl myself while I was home. Somebody threw a party and the whole family went. Arranged to see her next leave. We'll be getting a long one when we finally get our wings. Like Geoffrey.' He lit one of the cigarettes he'd started to smoke when he was away from home. 'How is Geoffrey, by the way? Has Edith finally collapsed into his arms?'

It was all uttered in jest, but it startled me how near the truth he was getting.

'Frank,' I said. 'When you stayed with us in the spring did you notice anything odd about Geoffrey and Edith?'

He grinned. 'Not odd. Pretty normal, I'd say. They were getting dewy-eyed about each other, that's all.'

It amazed me that I hadn't noticed.

'Was it that obvious?'

'It stuck out a mile.'

'Well, I'm blowed' – I was beginning to feel better suddenly – 'I never knew. It was Jane who told me.'

Frank grinned. 'Jane's a very perceptive young lady,' he said.

'She's only a kid, though.'

'She won't always be. I know a lot of girls who're still kids but I'm always nice to them in preparation for the future when they won't be.'

As I considered it all, I suddenly felt resentful. 'Why the blazes didn't you tell me?' I demanded, and he hooted with laughter.

'Because it's none of my business,' he said. 'I dropped a hint here and there, but there's none so blind as those who don't want to see.'

I had to agree. 'Perhaps you're right. I'll have to find a girl myself. I've noticed a few round Shoreham.'

Frank grinned again. 'You'll have to look slippy, old son,' he said. 'Because we're moving to Gosport.'

I stared at him. 'We are?'

'It's in orders. Both of us. They've changed the training. Advanced pupils are to go there to finish their courses in future. We're the first.'

I grabbed him and we did a little jig round the room, knocking over one of the beds and scattering equipment.

'When?' I asked breathlessly.

'Next Monday. I got it from one of the chaps, who got it from the sergeant in the orderly room…'

'Who picked it up from the adjutant, who got it from the mess cook,' I chanted.

He flung a boot at me. 'No, it's true! We're going there to be on hand for the formation of a new squadron.'

'How about Geoffrey?'

'His name's not down. But I see he's on the list as an instructor next week.'

'Well, I'm damned,' I said. 'That's going up in the world, isn't it? I expect it's just spare-time stuff till he goes to France.'

By the time we left for Gosport, I'd quite got over my annoyance about Edith and had accepted the situation between her and Geoffrey. I had suddenly decided, in fact, that I didn't wish to marry her even if she'd been free – at least not for some time. Frank and I had once discussed marriage at school and come to the conclusion that it seemed a pretty soppy institution and that we weren't very interested in it – though we'd accepted reluctantly that eventually most people did seem to get married. We'd settled finally for a date somewhere in our late twenties or early thirties, when we'd had a good look round the world. When that time came, I'd thought Edith would be a most suitable choice, simply because I was shy enough not to be very good with girls, unlike Frank who seemed to find them everywhere he went, and I'd decided it would be safer with someone I knew. 'The girl next door' had seemed an eminently suitable qualification.

–

The move to Gosport was a worrying prospect because at Shoreham we knew to a T just where to turn for a final approach, no matter which way the wind blew. It was either just beyond the bridge, just east of Lancing College, or the other side of the railway line, and the thought that all these points would have to be rediscovered all over again for a new field by a long period of trial and error was vaguely disturbing.

When we reached Gosport we found it didn't improve with acquaintance. We lived in rooms in the hollow ramparts of a disused star-shaped fort, and we found that in the mess there were far too many people already sporting wings who seemed unlikely ever to notice such small fry as we were, who'd only just gone solo. It was quite a come-down after being cock of the walk at Shoreham.

I didn't even like the look of the aeroplanes. There was only one Longhorn in sight and we'd got used to the comfortable motherly habits of the Longhorn. At Gosport our chief concern were Shorthorns, which had no tea-tray elevator in front to help us, or Caudrons, complete with twin wooden tail-booms and – most alarming of all – the engine in front, pulling the aircraft instead of pushing it. Never having flown a tractor aircraft, the very idea seemed impossible to me. How did you see past it? How could you judge your descent when you couldn't even see the earth? And a top speed of over seventy miles an hour seemed very alarming after the safe fifty-odd of the Longhorn.

Anxious for more experience before being pushed on to the newer machines, we huddled hopefully round the Longhorn, but I was taken firmly over to the Caudron by one of the instructors.

He told me to get in and try the cockpit for size. It was cramped and they locked you in with a piece of cowling which was bolted down on top of you. It seemed to me a little like being screwed down in a coffin. However, the instructor climbed in with me, and we took off, the instructor chatting in an amiable inconsequential fashion as he cut the engine with a switch at his side.

'Always needs left rudder,' he observed cheerfully, as though he were talking about the weather. 'And that's the throttle control position, but you can cut it back a little more for landing.'

I nodded, trying to remember it in case I was ever asked to take the machine up alone, and he switched on the engine again to demonstrate what he was talking about.

As we landed, he climbed out. I prepared to follow. 'Don't forget about the left rudder,' he said.

'No, I won't,' I promised.

'All right. Go on, take her up.'

I couldn't believe him, but the instructor, like Seago, was walking cheerfully away now, and before I knew what was happening, without really remembering any of the things he'd told me, I found the Caudron scuttling across the grass with me in control and, in a detached way, felt myself lifting her into the air.

Now that I had the controls, I realised that, despite the fact that they were stiffer because they worked by 'warping', the whole feel of the aircraft was more exciting. But there, nevertheless, smack in front of me, preventing me from seeing a thing, was the engine and the whirling propeller, while all round me seemed to be wood or fabric to obscure the view downwards.

I made it shakily back to earth between a line of trees that loomed up unexpectedly from below the nose when I was least expecting them and then I was down, putting the machine on to the grass with that uplifting gentleness that makes a perfect landing. While I was still trying to sort things out, the instructor's face appeared alongside me.

'Well done,' he said, so that my heart leapt with pride, and then he ruined it all by adding, 'We'll soon have you on half a dozen other types. You've obviously got the touch.'

It didn't appear to *me* that I'd got the touch, but certainly I seemed to have the edge on Frank, who always took just a little longer to get the hang of things than I did, and I began to realise at last that I'd discovered something that I could do better than other people. It seemed well worth concentrating on under the circumstances and I gave it all I'd got.

I did a few cross-country flights, had a minor forced landing in a field without harming myself or the aeroplane, and eventually got myself lost late at night returning from a cross-country to Haywards Heath and back. I put the machine down in a field north of Chichester without harming myself or breaking anything and, to my surprise, the instructor wasn't a bit perturbed. He even seemed pleased with me.

'I think you'd better try the BE,' he said. 'I think you're wasting your time on these things.'

Chapter 5

It was now late summer and as we drew towards the end of our courses we heard that the Widdows family had arrived in Littlehampton for a holiday before they got too involved with the harvesting. Old Widdows was a wealthy man and most of the work on his farm was done by hired labour, while he and the foreman made the decisions, so it wasn't as hard for him to get away as it was for some farmers.

They'd taken a house near the sea and Frank and I went over by train from Portsmouth to visit them. Jane – a brown, surprisingly interesting Jane – leapt at me rapturously, noisily demanding to know all there was to know about flying and offering to sew on my wings when I got them. Edith was more distant, friendly still and smiling, but definitely no longer interested in me. I was awkward with her, not quite knowing what to say but anxious to be as friendly as she was.

We swam and sailed the boat they'd hired, spending the whole of one long week-end with them, sleeping in a tent in the garden. Geoffrey came over on the Saturday by train from Shoreham and joined the party, but he and Edith didn't stay with the rest of us and wandered off on their own along the beach, outwardly looking for shells, but, in fact, just trying to be alone together.

That evening he and I sat on the beach throwing stones into the sea. Edith was helping her mother prepare the evening meal and Frank was playing a noisy game of tennis with Jane on the lawn behind us. For a long time Geoffrey was silent, then he coughed and moved restlessly.

'I'm thinking of getting engaged, Martin,' he said unexpectedly.

I looked round at him. 'To Edith?' I asked.

He smiled. 'Oh! So you know all about it?'

I gestured. 'It sticks out a mile,' I said off-handedly.

He shrugged. 'Oh! Well, I suppose it does. Do you mind?'

'Me? Why should I mind?'

He chuckled. 'Oh, nothing! Only you and Edith used to be as thick as thieves at one time. She said she was wondering how to tell you.'

'Tell her not to bother,' I said in a very adult, mature manner. 'Tell her I knew all about it and just kept out of the way.'

Geoffrey grinned. 'That's pretty thoughtful of you,' he said. 'Of course, we're keeping it to ourselves for a bit. Her people know, naturally – they must have guessed – but it's not official. You don't feel left out of it?'

'Me?' I made a big show of indifference and understanding. 'Of course not.'

Geoffrey smiled. 'There's always Jane,' he pointed out.

'Don't make me laugh,' I said.

'More your age. More your type, come to that.'

'She'll be all right,' I said knowingly, 'when she grows up a bit.'

He looked gravely at me. 'You'd be surprised how quickly they manage it,' he said. 'It startled *me* a bit.'

He was staring at me, a half-smile on his face and looking as handsome as the devil in the fading light, and suddenly I felt terribly warm towards him. In spite of his teasing, he'd always been the sort of older brother that most people hoped for. He'd kept an eye on me at school, and stopped people bullying me. He'd shown me how to do things and helped me when I didn't do them well. And, though he was as different as chalk from cheese from me with his music and painting and his habit of slipping out of your grasp at times into imaginations of his own that left you alone and suddenly lost, we had always been very close to each other.

'I always did say you were a bit slow on the uptake,' he said.

'What do you mean?' I demanded, despite my affection for him as edgy as I always was when he teased me.

'Oh, it'll dawn on you one day,' he said.

He seemed to be on the point of slipping out of my grasp even then and I tried to hang on to him with some mundane comment.

'I should think you feel a shelf higher than everybody else at the moment, don't you?' I said.

He looked hard at me and smiled. 'That just about sums it up,' he agreed. 'I didn't realise you had such a gift for seeing things.'

'I'm not as slow as some people imagine.'

We talked happily for a while longer, then something that had been worrying me for some time came to the surface. I probed gently. 'How'll you feel when you go to France?' I asked.

Geoffrey gave me a strange look. 'Perhaps I shan't go to France,' he said.

I stared at him, frowning. It was as I'd suspected. He was still instructing at Shoreham when others in his group had already gone abroad and I'd thought about it a lot.

'Won't go to France?' I said cautiously.

'I don't particularly want to,' he admitted. 'Especially now. They tell me I'm a good instructor and that, if I want to, I can stay at Shoreham, turning out pilots.'

I was vaguely shocked. The whole point of becoming a pilot had been to go to France and fly against the Germans.

'But you don't want to do that, do you?' I said.

'Why not?' He smiled. 'For heaven's sake, you young fire-eater, it's as much a part of the war effort as shooting down Germans, isn't it?'

It was something that hadn't occurred to me. 'Yes, I suppose it is,' I said reluctantly. 'But, good Lord, fancy not wanting to go to France!'

He smiled. 'I've been *once*,' he pointed out. 'And shed my drop of blood. And things are a bit different for me now.'

–

After supper I was sitting on the front wall of the house, staring at the sea. Jane had vanished into the town with Frank and I was feeling a little out of it. Frank always seemed to be able to think of things to do and Jane was never slow to join in, and I was brooding a little on my aloneness when I realised that Edith was alongside me.

'Hello, Martin,' she said.

I moved over to make room for her and she sat down beside me.

'Geoffrey tells me you know about us,' she said.

For a moment I was at a loss what to say. How did you reply to such a question when it concerned your elder brother and the girl you'd thought ever since adolescence you were in love with?

'Yes,' I said. 'He told me. But I knew already, of course,' I added quickly.

'You're not hurt?'

'Not a bit.' It was reasonably true by this time. 'I'm pleased for you, Edith. Old Geoff's rather a good chap, really, even though he's my brother.'

'Yes,' she said, blushing a little, her head down. 'He is rather. At least, I think so. We shall make it official when Geoffrey knows what his future is. I believe he's told you what his plans are.'

'Yes. He's told me.'

'He had a feeling that you didn't entirely approve.'

'I wouldn't have thought that what I felt mattered to Geoff,' I said.

She smiled, turning the full glow of her large dark eyes on me. 'You'd be surprised how highly he regards your opinion.'

It was news to me but it was a pleasant thought all the same.

'You see, he's thinking of me,' she went on, as though trying to explain Geoffrey's unexpected line of action and eager to have me on their side. 'I probably influenced him. He wasn't sure whether his duty lay with a squadron in France or at home with me.'

'I should tell him, Edith,' I said, 'that the best thing he can do is stay here and take good care of you.'

I didn't honestly mean what I said because I was still in that euphoric state about the war when I thought every man's duty was to stand up to the Germans in France, but Edith seemed satisfied that I'd put my approval into words, whether I meant it or not.

'I'll tell him what you said,' she smiled. 'He'll feel better about staying at home then.'

'Yes' – I didn't know what to do with my hands and flapped them in a vague gesture – 'well, congratulations, anyway, for when it happens. Just in case I've been posted to France by then.'

'Thanks, Martin.'

'And the wedding?' I went on. 'When will that be? Or haven't you got around to discussing that yet?'

She smiled, a mature, proud smile as though she were sure of herself and of Geoffrey. 'Oh, yes,' she said. 'We've discussed it all right. We thought at first that with the war…'

'I shouldn't let that interfere,' I said quickly, suddenly realising that if they did get married I'd probably be able to get leave out of it.

'No, we won't.' She looked up at me again with that new adult womanly way that made me feel an immature schoolboy. 'We decided not to. I hope you'll be best man, Martin. I'd like you to be best man more than anyone else.'

'I'll probably make a mess of it, but I'll try.'

When she'd gone, Jane appeared. 'What were you two up to?' she asked.

'Talking about them getting engaged,' I said. 'They want me to be best man.'

She cocked a leg over the wall and sat alongside me. 'Why not?' she said. 'You'd do it rather well, I should think.'

'Me?' The moon had come up and was hanging over the sea like a yellow orange and from inside the house I could hear the tinkle of a piano on the gramophone. I guessed that Geoffrey and Edith were listening to it and holding hands while Mr and Mrs Widdows sat in the kitchen keeping out of the way. 'I never did anything very well.'

'Frank says you're not bad at flying,' Jane pointed out.

I shrugged. 'It'll probably be different when the shooting starts.'

She made disbelieving noises. 'I think you make a jolly good soldier.'

I shrugged again. I always felt that in uniform I looked like something left over from the quartermaster's store, and I knew mine was an unprepossessing face, with ordinary features and ordinary hair.

'Not me,' I said. 'Frank's more the type.'

She shook her head. 'Don't you believe it, Martin,' she said. 'I know no one more fitted for waging war than Martin Falconer.'

What she said pleased me and for a moment I felt a hell of a fellow, then she quite destroyed the moment.

'But looking round at you all,' she said bluntly, 'I think what an awful waste it all is. Soon there'll be nobody left in England worth knowing. I think I'll marry a grocer.'

–

I made my first flight in the BE2a. It was a slender machine that was actually much more sturdy than it looked, but it had a curiously exposed engine which seemed to have been stuck on the front as an afterthought, and a rudder which sat on the stern rather like the rudder of a racing shell, as though it didn't really belong to the machine at all. It also had a huge wooden skid between the wheels which was supposed to stop it standing on its nose and a ninety-horse engine which was reputed to carry it along at sixty-odd miles an hour. It seemed a terrifyingly modern aircraft, and was reputed to be quick to spin. This was rather alarming because none of us was still very sure what a spin was like or what you did to get out of one, because no one seemed to have survived one to tell us. The rumour went that if you did find yourself in one – provided you could recognise it, of course – all you had to do was cross your controls and put the stick forward so that the spin became a simple dive. It seemed far too easy to be true, however, and the prospect still remained a nightmare.

The BE was heavy on the controls, but it was said that one had actually been looped by some iron-nerved daredevil – though, so the story went, he hadn't bothered to repeat the experience.

I was allowed by this time to fly not only when the flag was stirring on the pole but even when it stood out straight or the air was bumpy with heat. I flew inland and out over the Channel, banking the machine steeply when I turned so that I felt a real daredevil. I carried my first passengers, cheerful uninitiated young men who were happily unaware of my inexperience as they enjoyed the view of the Solent from the air. I had a minor crash that wiped away the undercarriage and saw several more, none of them messy or fatal, and began at last to feel quite expert.

Frank found a new girl friend and I kept bumping into them in cafés with their heads close together. Jane was talking of leaving school and getting a job, and Geoffrey had done exactly what he had said he would and had made sure he would remain at Shoreham for the time being. He occasionally flew in to Gosport with a pupil or as a passenger, a little quieter than before and almost as though he were apologising to me – me, his younger brother! – for opting out of the war.

'How's it going with you?' he asked, and I was proud to announce we were almost through. There wasn't much ahead of us now before we could put up the coveted wings, and we already felt prepared for anything.

'I wish they'd get on with things a bit, though,' Frank said impatiently. 'We've learned all we can.'

Geoffrey smiled, his eyes pitying. 'Don't you believe it, Frank,' he said. 'When you leave here you've only just started.'

–

We weren't quite sure what he meant and, still flying 'cross-countries', waited patiently for our final tests. Every day now we stared at the notice board for our names on orders to go to Upavon. The summer was almost gone but still they didn't appear.

'They've forgotten us,' Frank wailed. 'As usual! The war'll be over before we get in it. I expect they've lost our papers or something equally stupid.'

While we were still waiting, Geoffrey appeared again. He was flying as passenger to some officer on the staff of the Flying Corps, who was piloting a brand-new BE2c. This was the machine I'd lost my heart to at Shoreham, in the early days of training, and was a big improvement on the 2a I was flying. Its fin made the rudder seem more part of the machine and there was no sign of the skid. The engine looked bigger, too, because they'd added a cowling underneath and it was said to be capable of ninety miles an hour.

'Wouldn't mind flying one of those,' Frank said longingly. 'What's it feel like? Riding on a rocket?'

Geoffrey smiled. 'Only the bigwigs and the people in France can get these machines,' he pointed out.

'Is *your* chap a bigwig?'

'Not half. He's new to piloting, though, and I've been sent along with him to make sure he doesn't lose the way. There are quite a lot of these chaps in the Flying Corps. They joined from the Army and they've now got senior jobs. But they felt they ought to learn to fly and so they did, though I think a lot of them are better administrators than they are pilots.'

I asked him how Edith was and he grinned happily.

'She's coming down to Worthing today,' he said. 'She'll be there when I get back. I've booked her in at a hotel for the week-end. It'll be nice to have her around, and the C.O.'s asked us to dine with him. I'm one of his bright boys these days, you see.'

'Fixed the date, yet?' I asked.

'Not yet. But it's official now. I bought her a ring.'

'If it were me,' I said, 'I'd marry her. I'd want to make sure of her. Tie her down a bit.'

He laughed. 'That's the difference between you and me,' he observed. 'You go bull-headed at the things you want. I have a little more finesse.'

'Finesse won't be much good,' I advised, 'if you turn up one day and find she's arranged to marry another chap.'

He frowned. 'It's not as easy as that,' he said. 'I have to think of Edith and there's a war on. I wouldn't want her to be left a widow or anything like that.'

'Oh, for heaven's sake,' I said. 'You're not likely to.'

I felt he was slipping out of my grasp, as he often did, and his eyes became far away.

'Aren't I?' he said. 'I'd say there was always a possibility, though, wouldn't you?'

'Not on your life,' I said. 'You're a good pilot.'

He suddenly became angry. 'Oh, for God's sake, Martin,' he said brusquely. 'Wake up. Face facts. You're still a starry-eyed boy. "It's a wonderful war. Our duty's to kill Germans – by the thousand, if possible. We're the best pilots in the world and we fly the best aeroplanes." Well, we don't. Some of us are indifferent and some of the machines we fly are quite dreadful. As for the war – well, the sooner it ends the better, as far as I'm concerned, because I for one don't enjoy the thought of killing – whether they're Germans or not.'

It was an unexpected outburst and he stalked away, leaving me troubled and bewildered. Later, however, he seemed to recover and at lunch in the mess we sat side by side, listening while the great man who'd flown the BE2c held forth on future plans for the R.F.C. It seemed to me that the aircraft he was talking about for the following year were horrifyingly fast.

After lunch he went out to the field, intending to take off for Filton, and he and Geoffrey stood by the machine, fastening their helmets. As Geoffrey settled himself in the passenger's place under the wings, he saw me standing among the crowd and waved cheerfully, then the great man gave the engine full throttle and they took off.

The machine rose quickly, the wings transparent in the glare of the sun, then, while we were all still waving, I heard the engine cough harshly, twice, like gunshots, and the exhaust roar became a broken clattering.

When the nose dipped, the BE was only about two hundred feet up and it seemed to hang in the air over a group of houses. There was a good chance of hitting one of them if the pilot tried to put his nose down at once to land, as we'd been taught, and the great man made the elementary mistake of trying to turn back down-wind.

'No!' I shouted instinctively, aware of Frank alongside me with his mouth open. 'Don't turn back!'

The sun glowed through the translucent wings as the machine turned, held course for a while, then turned again.

'He's going to get away with it,' Frank said. Inexperienced as we were, we could see the terrible risk the great man was taking.

'He's losing flying speed,' someone behind me said, and even as he spoke I saw the BE stall. The pilot was just trying to make his final turn over the sheds when the machine appeared to slide sideways along the length of its wing. The nose went down and, though I'd never seen one, I recognised the movement at once as the first turn of a spin.

The edge of the wing caught the roof of the shed and I saw fragments fly off, then the engine – surprisingly enough, because it had seemed to be dead – caught again, gave a scream of terror as the machine disappeared, then faded once more in a series of diminishing pops. As the machine vanished, there was a tremendous crash.

There was a stunned silence and I noticed the birds singing, then we were all running as hard as we could go. As we rounded the shed, I saw the BE was now no more than a splintered mass of spruce and torn fabric with its smoking engine crooked in its housing. The pilot was trying to scramble clear already and I could see Geoffrey's arms moving as he pushed his way through the collapsed wings.

'Thank God,' I said, thinking curiously of Edith.

Even as we approached, however, I saw a puff of smoke beneath the engine. A mechanic had reached the wreck by this time and was trying to help the pilot out, but the exploding petrol hurled him backwards, yelling and beating at his blazing overalls. The pilot had fallen clear with him, yelling like the mechanic, and was immediately seized and rolled on the ground to put out the flames that were flickering along his back.

'Geoffrey!' The word came in a breathless scream and I was startled to realise it was uttered in my own voice.

I could see Geoffrey still moving among the furnace glow of the flames and I jumped forward to go to his help. Frank grabbed my arm and hung on to me desperately, dragging me round.

'Martin, no!' he yelled. 'It's too late!'

'Let me go!' I said, my eyes still on Geoffrey's feebly moving form, then, as Frank swung me away, I caught a glimpse of his arm in the air and a doubled fist, and lights flashed before my eyes.

When I came round I was lying on the grass by the corner of the hangar out of sight of the crash. Frank was kneeling over me with a couple of other men, his face strained, his eyes troubled.

'Martin,' he said. 'I'm sorry! I had to do something!'

I pushed myself to a sitting position and looked around, suddenly remembering Geoffrey. 'Where's Geoff?' I said.

One of the other men dragged me to my feet and I saw then that it was one of the instructors. The third man was another pupil.

'Get him away from here,' the instructor said sharply.

'Get him to his room. And see that he stays there.'

I felt numb, still seeing in my mind's eye that violent flower of flame, still curiously thinking of Edith. The pupil hanging on to my right arm was mumbling to himself. 'Oh God,' he kept saying, and in the end I wrenched my arm away.

'I'll manage on my own,' I said.

Frank looked troubled. 'You can't go back there, Martin,' he said.

'I'm not going back,' I told him, and marched on alone. Frank gave the other pupil a quick glance then he jerked his head to send him away and followed me on his own. Someone gave me a drink of whisky that made me cough and splutter, then the commanding officer sent for me, and said how sorry he was.

'This is a rotten business, Falconer,' he said. 'Is there anything we can do?'

I couldn't help thinking of Edith waiting in the hotel in Worthing for Geoffrey to return, dressed in her best and excited at the prospect of being with him.

'My brother's fiancée's come down to see him,' I said. 'She's in Worthing. Someone ought to tell her.'

He stared at me, frowning. 'Think *you* can handle it?' he asked.

'I think so, sir.'

'Would you like that friend of yours – Griffiths – to go with you?'

'It might help, sir.'

He nodded. 'I'll arrange it at once. Report to me when you get back. Make it tomorrow if you can. The funeral will be the following afternoon.'

'And Falconer' – I stopped in the doorway as the C.O.'s voice came again – 'try to persuade the young lady not to attend, if you can. In cases like this I think it's best.'

Half an hour later Frank and I were heading in the C.O.'s car for the station. Neither of us spoke and we sat in silence as the train left Fareham and passed through Havant. It was a hot summer evening such as you can only get on the south coast, gold-bronze-yellow with the whitewashed walls glowing in the light of the sinking sun. Frank was watching me, but he was wisely saying nothing because he knew I didn't want to talk, unobtrusive but very close to me in his friendship and sympathy. Finally, as we passed through Chichester, he coughed.

'Anything you want me to do, Martin,' he said, 'I'll do it. Any way you like. I mean' – he moved his hands in a helpless gesture – 'I don't know how you're proposing to set about this thing but if you'd like me to see her first...'

'No.' I shook my head. 'I'll see her. I think it's better that way. But I'd like you to be there in the hotel in case I need you.'

He nodded and gave me a small twisted smile. 'Yes, of course. Anything you like.'

We couldn't find a taxi at Worthing and we had to hire a landau with a decrepit horse between the shafts, passing holiday-makers who were taking the evening sun. They seemed to think we were on holiday, too, and waved to us and one or two girls smiled.

At the hotel we stood on the pavement looking at each other, both of us wondering what to do next, and I remembered that only a few months before I'd still been a schoolboy with nothing more serious to worry about than cricket and football scores.

Frank's eyes were on me. 'Shall I wait in the hall?' he asked.

I nodded. 'You'll probably have to telephone to Fynling, I expect,' I said.

'I'll just hang around, then, till you want me.'

I gave him a grateful look, jerked my jacket straight and swallowed hard. I felt awful and terribly young, still a starry-eyed boy, as Geoffrey had said.

I found Edith sitting in the lounge by the open French windows. She was wearing a white lacy dress and white stockings and shoes and a shady straw hat with flowers on it. She was holding her left hand in the way so many newly engaged girls hold them – so she could see her new ring – and I could see the sun glinting on the stone.

As she saw me, she put down her book and rose, smiling, an expression of delight on her face.

'Martin! How nice to see you!'

Then she realised that I hadn't returned her smile and her eyes went strangely dead and empty. 'What is it?' she said in a low voice. 'Has something happened to Geoffrey?'

'Oh God,' I thought, 'how do I do this? How can I put it so that it isn't too painful?'

'Yes,' I said. 'There was an accident. A flying accident.'

'Is he all right?' She had sat down again abruptly, her fingers picking at the arm of the chair.

I shook my head numbly. 'No,' I said. 'He was killed.'

She didn't say anything for a moment, lifting her hands to her mouth and pressing them tightly over her lips as though she were trying to stop herself crying out loud in her anguish.

'Oh God!' she whispered.

'Edith,' I pleaded. 'What can I do?'

She shook her head, not saying anything, and I was aware of people staring at us.

'He couldn't have suffered at all, Edith,' I lied.

Still she didn't speak, her eyes staring at me as though they were seeing straight through me.

'It was over in a second.'

She spoke at last. 'It doesn't make any difference either way now, does it?' she said in a cold distant voice, and for a moment I thought she loathed me.

Then, suddenly, her face crumpled up and her body wilted and she broke into sobs that shook her whole frame. As I bent over her, at a loss what to do, Frank appeared alongside with a glass in his hand.

'Better drink this, Edith,' he said gently. 'It's brandy.'

—

We got her to her room and Frank telephoned the police at Fynling. Some time later my father rang back. It was as difficult as telling Edith, because the telegram hadn't yet arrived about Geoffrey and I had to break the news. My father's voice came, stiff with trying to hang on to his emotions.

'I'll let your mother and Edith's parents know,' he said. 'I'll ring you again as soon as I can.'

Frank and I stayed with Edith, both of us wretchedly unhappy because by this time the full shock of what had happened had hit her and she couldn't stop crying. The hotel staff were kind and did all they could to help. After a while my father rang back once more.

'The family's on their way,' he said. 'They'll be there by midnight. Can you hang on?'

'Yes, we'll stay with her till they arrive.' I paused. 'How about Mother?' I added. 'How did she take it?'

My father's voice came back, brusque and sharp. 'How did you think she'd take it, boy?' he said.

I felt hurt, because I was feeling the same way they were, but then I realised there was no implied criticism, and that my father had only been trying to keep his own emotions in check.

I was about to put the phone down when my father's voice came again, anxious this time. 'Martin!'

'Yes? I'm still here.'

'What about the funeral? Should I do anything?'

'The Flying Corps'll take care of it, Father.'

'I think we can be down there on the morning train.'

'No!' I didn't want them near the place because I was afraid they might find out exactly what had happened. 'No, I should stay there, Father. And keep Mother there. It's best.'

'Why? What happened to Geoffrey?'

I told him. 'I don't want Mother wanting to see him or anything like that.'

I heard him sigh down the long length of the wire. 'Very well,' he said. 'I'm sure you're right. But she'll want to come and I shan't be able to stop her.'

I sat with Edith, waiting in the silent room long after dark and listening to the pathetic little mewing noises she made in her grief, until finally the ordeal was ended by a small scratching noise on the door.

It was Edith's parents, their expressions tragic. Behind them I saw Jane, her face frozen and empty. She managed a twisted smile at me as I slipped out. I tried to offer my condolences but they hardly seemed to hear and it seemed time for us to leave.

'We'll have to be going back to camp, Janey,' I said. 'Will you be all right now?'

She nodded. 'We'll be all right,' she said. 'You'd better get back to your war.'

I didn't even notice that everybody seemed to be taking it out on me.

When I went downstairs Frank was still waiting in the hall and I was so glad to see him I felt tears come to my eyes. He rose to his feet, his eyes questioning.

'It's all right,' I said. 'She'll be all right now. We can go.'

He said nothing, but pushed a glass across to me. It was full of amber liquid.

'Better drink that first,' he said.

'What is it?'

'Brandy. I should think it's a treble by the size of it. The hotel's quite expert at this sort of thing now. It's happened before – at Shoreham.'

I stared at the glass. 'I've never drunk brandy in my life,' I said.

He stared at me sombrely. 'I think you'd better drink this one,' he advised.

–

We got back to camp by breakfast-time the next day and went to the C.O.'s office to report.

'It must have been a wretched business for you,' he said, then he became brisk and businesslike, as though he were anxious to get on with things.

'I think the best thing to do is get yourself immersed in work,' he advised. 'It'll take your mind off things. Besides, after an affair like that, I don't like you chaps not flying. It's too upsetting.'

He seemed a bit cold-hearted at the time, but he was right, of course, and I threw myself into work immediately to stop myself thinking.

They held the funeral the following afternoon. Edith and her family and my parents turned up in spite of my warning, but I managed to avoid seeing them for too long, claiming that I was on duty, and the C.O. told them very little.

I stood straight-faced with Frank while a volley was fired at the graveside. The ceremony all seemed a bit pointless to me because it didn't do either Geoffrey or Edith much good, but suddenly I began to see what Geoffrey had been getting at that time when he'd said the war wasn't a football match.

'People sometimes get killed,' he'd said. 'It isn't just flags and trumpets. War's rather a messy business and, for some, pretty painful and inglorious.'

Frank and I saw my parents and Edith's family to the station and by the grace of God there was little time to talk. The train came in soon after we arrived and my mother was in no state to ask questions. As they climbed into the carriage for London, Edith turned to me. She seemed to have her grief well in hand by now, and although she was pale-faced and taut-featured, her eyes were dry.

'Thank you, Martin,' she said. 'And bless you for coming to tell me. I don't know what I'd have done if it had been a stranger.'

My mother held me close and I felt her tears on my cheek, then my father bundled her into the carriage and as the train left I saw Jane's face, white and tragic, at the window. As they slipped away down the platform I felt an immense sense of relief that it was all over.

-

We'd almost finished our courses now and by rights were entitled to leave, but, deliberately, I think, the commanding officer kept us on the camp, and it was nearly a month later before we got home to Norwich.

I still felt numb, but no one made any concessions for me and there was more work on a BE and an Avro, a tremendously stable machine which was reputed to have been once started by accident as I'd started the Caudron, had taken off on its own and, chased by the pilot in a motor-car, had finally landed itself without damage. We did what passed for formation flying and the beginnings of artillery spotting and passed our tests in aerodynamics, radio and Morse. Finally, we went to the Central Flying School at Upavon to be passed out as pilots.

It all turned out to be much easier than we'd expected and we found we'd passed. We were no longer fledglings. We were pilots and as such entitled at last to wear wings.

It seemed an anticlimax, however, with Geoffrey's death, and strange to think we'd be going to France without him. In our occupation with work we'd had little time to remember him, though, and I realised how right the C.O. had been.

Leave was granted at last and since we were to go overseas immediately on our return, Frank came home with me before going on to Leicester, to say goodbye to my parents. He'd stayed with us often and felt he ought to see them before going on to his own people.

He spent the first night with us, a rather subdued night because my mother still hadn't really got over Geoffrey's death and moved about the house with a crucified look on her face, quite unable to push from her mind the fact that her elder son was dead. She hadn't touched his room and it was exactly as he'd left it – rather like a shrine. The commanding officer had been careful not to mention in his talk to her the exact manner of Geoffrey's death and we were careful not to tell her.

'It was instantaneous,' Frank insisted, his face tense with the earnestness of his lie. 'He couldn't have felt a thing, Mrs Falconer.'

When I'd seen Frank off at the station in Norwich I caught the next train back to Fynling, but, instead of facing my mother, I felt I had to see Edith to try to give her some comfort.

As usual the door was opened by Jane. She'd got rid of her plaits and seemed more grown-up suddenly.

'Sorry,' she said briskly. 'No maids. All on war work. I've taken over. I've left school now.'

'What are you going to do, Jane?' I said, aware already of the difference in her.

'Don't want any pilots, do you?' she asked. 'Wouldn't mind doing that.'

I managed a stiff smile and she shrugged. 'Well, what else is there?' she asked. 'Everybody who's anything of a man's joined the forces, and there's nothing but women and girls around here. I think I'll get a job. You won't see me for dust, in fact, if I get a chance.'

'What are you thinking of doing?'

'I wish I knew. Everybody seems to frown on girls working. I think I'll learn to use a typewriting machine and get a job in Norwich. There's bound to be a shortage of help if things go on the way they are.'

We talked for a little longer, then I asked cautiously about Edith.

'She's out,' Jane said.

'Out?' I was a little startled. I'd half expected her to appear tragic-faced in black. 'What doing?'

'She got a job,' she said. 'She's offered to go nursing and she's at the hospital. She's still learning, but she'll be all right in time.'

I paused. 'How about Geoffrey?' I asked. 'How did she take it?'

'She cried,' Jane said bluntly. 'What did you expect?'

I felt I wasn't doing very well and cursed myself for my clumsiness. 'How is she now?'

'She's recovering,' she said. 'There's a young doctor at the hospital pretty interested in her. She's seeing a lot of him.'

My face fell. '*Seeing a lot of him!*' I felt somehow that this was sheer heartlessness. Jane stared at me.

'What did you expect?' she said. 'Weeping won't bring Geoffrey back, will it?'

'No, but…'

'But what? She's got to go on living, hasn't she? Even though people are getting killed, life doesn't stop.'

'No, I suppose not.'

Then her face softened and I realised that the hard matter-of-factness was all put on to help steel herself against what had suddenly probably seemed a very brutal and relentless world.

'It's no good thinking badly of her, Martin,' she said. 'She can't just sit in a dark corner for the rest of her life mourning Geoffrey. I think she thought the world of him, as a matter of fact, but that's all over now, isn't it? She's got to face things, and she's doing the best she can.'

I felt faintly humble in front of such common sense. 'Yes,' I said. 'I see that, Janey. It shook me a bit at first, but of course you're quite right.'

'If *you* got killed,' Jane said gravely, 'I'd want to go and hide myself, Martin. But I wouldn't. I'd go out and do something as hard as I could, so I'd forget it.'

'Yes.' There wasn't much difference, really, between what she and Edith were doing and what Frank and I, encouraged by the C.O., had been doing at Gosport. The only antidote to tragedy *was* work.

Suddenly I knew with certainty that this was something I was going to have to face up to more than once in the future. Our world – that place of warmth, security and stability – had started to fall apart on the day the first shot of the war was fired. It was vanishing now – though we didn't know it yet – in a welter of unreason and misery. And, though I still didn't know what we were in for, I knew it was going to involve us with death.

Some of that starry-eyed excitement Geoffrey had accused me of had already gone, though I'm not sure that perhaps it wasn't a better way to go to war than the brand of romantic disillusionment Geoffrey had acquired. Doubtless he had once felt as I did and doubtless I'd end up feeling as he had, but I certainly wasn't afraid for myself. As he'd pointed out, it was always the other man you expected to be killed, never yourself – though I knew I was going to have to face grim facts, nevertheless. Before long Frank and I would be in France and there'd be no backing out then.

Chapter 6

St Omer. The name had a sort of magic because it was the Royal Flying Corps' main aircraft depot in France, the place through which all machines had to pass on their way to the front. Squadrons formed in England had to report there before going on to the front-line aerodromes. Ferry pilots, flying machines backwards and forwards, were always in and out. All new machines were assembled and tested there before being sent to the squadrons to replace those damaged beyond repair or lost over enemy-occupied territory. Here were tested engines, guns, compasses. Here were issued stores and spare parts, and here captured enemy aircraft were flown for comparison with our own. Here also was the headquarters of the General Officer Commanding.

From St Omer, Frank and I travelled by Crossley tender southwards and eastwards towards the area of the fighting. I was already conscious of a change in me. At home, with Geoffrey's death, there had been a difference in attitudes towards me. While we had all deferred to Geoffrey as the clever one of the family, the intelligent one from whom big things were expected, now there was only me and I realised I had taken up a new position with regard to my parents. I could hardly replace Geoffrey for intelligence, charm and potential, but now I was all there was left, and they'd paid attention to me and cared for my wishes with a new sad affection because they were afraid that I, too, might die.

As for me, I knew I could no longer lean on Geoffrey, no longer look to him for an example. I was on my own now. I had to make up my own mind, work out my own standards of behaviour and honour and decency and try to live up to them without any encouragement from an elder brother.

I'd seen Edith before I'd left to meet Frank in London for the Dover train. She'd been quieter than I'd remembered her, but prettier, too. I'd met her quite by accident in the street in Norwich, and she'd been walking with the doctor who Jane had said was seeing a lot of her. He was tall and fair and good-looking and I'd been struck by the fact that he was surprisingly like Geoffrey. Then I'd realised that this was probably the whole point of their closeness and regarded it as a compliment to our family and my brother that Edith's second choice was so much like the first.

We'd been polite with each other, but, with her new status and with Geoffrey dead, I'd been aware that things were already different between us. She'd no longer had any allegiance to our family and in fact had already been turning towards the family of this stranger. I'd no longer blamed her, however, and, because she'd seemed so tranquil, so calm, I'd known she'd done what was right in deciding to live despite Geoffrey's death. I could only wish her luck.

'You can't blame her,' Jane had said defiantly when I'd told her. 'She's still entitled to a future, in spite of this beastly war.'

She'd seemed startled when I'd agreed with her and, because the weather was good, we'd got the boat out and sailed down to Acle Bridge and back. My mind was still occupied with that last sail in the yellow light of late summer as the Crossley drew to a stop in the town where wing headquarters was situated. The wind had been perfect and we'd bought a loaf and butter and cheese and bottled beer, and, by a tacit understanding, had never mentioned Geoffrey and Edith. It had been a perfect day, with hardly any words between us — just a quiet pleasure in the boat and the wind and the weather.

Frank nudged me and I realised I'd still been busy thinking about it.

'Time to report for the final posting,' he said.

In the afternoon we set off again for our squadron, which was stationed at a place called Illy. The year was still warm and the dusty roads took us beneath the double rows of poplars as we began to head east and north.

We passed through a small market town, full of French farmers bringing their produce to sell, stout women in black doing their shopping, and a few neat girls carrying baskets. There were troops everywhere, both in French blue and British khaki. Long cavalcades of cavalry, stirring up the dust as they clattered past. Hordes of marching men, bent under the enormous weights they carried on their backs, brown-faced and sturdy, swinging eastwards, as though they could march all day despite the loads they bore. A few of them called out good-natured jeers as we roared past in the Crossley.

The gunfire, which we'd heard first in St Omer, and again a little louder at wing headquarters, coming in fits and starts to make us whisper as we tried to listen for it above the talk, now came in a steady rumbling and muttering in some nameless threat from just beyond the dusty horizon.

We stopped at last alongside an orchard where we could see wooden huts with oiled-silk windows. One of them, obviously the squadron office, had a fluttering blue flag outside and a Le Rhône cylinder hanging on a little gibbet for what we later learned was a gas alarm. The other huts, set further back among the trees, had been labelled by wags with names as though they were public houses – the Pig and Whistle, the Dove and Rumpety, the Bomb and Zeppelin. They varied in wit and cleverness, but it was clear the names gave the occupants a small nostalgic feeling of home. We were directed to the Pig and Whistle, a bare empty hut containing four bunks.

'We had a bad time last week, sir,' the sergeant pointed out as he backed out of the door. 'We lost two machines.'

'Shot down?' we asked at once.

'Bless you, no, sir,' he said, as though that was the last thing that could happen. 'Nothing like *that*. One of 'em had to come down in

Hunland, sir. Dud engine. Crew were taken prisoners. The Germans dropped a note. The other one crash-landed in a cross-wind. Nothing serious. Broken collarbone, that's all. You'll find the flight commander by the hangars, sir.'

The flight commander reminded me a little of Seago at Shoreham, a tall spare young man wearing a stock and canvas leggings and carrying a riding whip. Quite a lot of the pilots were cavalrymen who'd graduated to flying when machine-guns and trenches had brought their work of reconnaissance by horse to a full stop. Their knowledge had soon made them observers, and a few of them by this time had progressed into the ranks of the pilots.

He acknowledged our quivering salutes with a vague movement of the riding crop, blinking a little as though he were startled to be so earnestly greeted.

'Names? Griffiths. Falconer. Any relation of the Leicester Falconers? No, I don't suppose you are. I'm Sykes. Most people call me Bill. After Dickens, shouldn't wonder.'

He seemed just too vague to be true but I noticed he had an M.C. beneath his wings and assumed that his airy indifference was all put on

– the old cavalry attitude, that the war was just a vulgar brawl and that the cavalry were there merely to lend a little tone. The war *had* to seem a bit of a bore, because the boredom saved talking about it too much.

'See that you give the usual cheer-me-up particulars to the office,' he advised. 'Religion. Next of kin. Favourite flowers. Nature of grandmother's rheumatism. All helps.' He seemed an amiable young man not prepared to take life very seriously, a thing I'd already noticed about most experienced people in the Flying Corps. They flew their unstable, inflammable machines with an air of indifference, and most of them seemed to set off for the war as though they were going to a football match. It was an attitude Frank and I had begun to cultivate ourselves.

'How many flying hours?' Sykes went on.

'Thirty-two, sir,' I said.

'Not much, is it?' He smiled. 'Ah, well, we'll see what we can do. Flown BEs? You have?' He seemed pleased and his vague expression lit up. 'Jolly good. We'll see that you fly a lot more. Come and see me in the morning when you've got settled in.'

We threw him up another salute, stiff with the earnestness of it. He acknowledged it with another embarrassed movement of the riding crop.

'Don't need to go in for too much of that nonsense,' he advised wearily. 'Some squadrons do, but we find here that we manage to be just as efficient without it. Just the C.O. That's all. Always the C.O.'

He wandered off, vague, casual, blank-faced, and we stared at each other.

'Well,' Frank said. 'He makes the war seem like a rather tedious tea-party, doesn't he?'

We reported to the office, as suggested, then wandered round the workshops, stores, tents and transport lines, finding our way about. A few people spoke to us, but for the most part we were treated with the same friendly indifference we'd been used to at Shoreham.

The field was a sloping area of blackened stubble, where the corn stooks had been piled in the hedgerows and left to rot. Trees at one end had been lopped to make it easier to get in, but it was still not my idea of an ideal landing ground. It looked too short and was too narrow at one end, and the perimeter was well studded with awkwardly placed barns. Still, I decided, there was a war on and we had to put up with this sort of thing.

When we'd finished unpacking and found our way about, we heard an engine start up and went outside to see a BE taking off. It lifted neatly over the trees towards the east, a smart flimsy-looking white aeroplane, the rondels on the upper wing silhouetted through the fabric against the structure as it passed over us against the sun.

'Wonder who's in it?' Frank said.

At dinner in the mess that night the talk was all about aeroplanes and I realised that, despite their casual air, these young men around me were all dedicated fliers eager to find out everything they could about a profession that was still only half explored. Halfway through the meal we heard an aeroplane engine buzzing overhead and then, as the throttle was closed, the 'whoosh' as the machine passed over the mess to land. After a while Sykes arrived. He sat down, quietly drank his soup and took a sip of wine.

'What was it like, Bill?' one of the other flight commanders asked.

Sykes looked up. 'Bit bad-tempered at times,' he said. Then I realised that he'd been the pilot of the white BE which had taken off earlier and he'd come up against enemy gunfire, and after dinner we went down to the hangar to have a look at his machine. The riggers were working over gashes in the wings and fuselage.

'"Bad-tempered at times",' Frank said thoughtfully. 'It looks to me as though people were throwing things.'

That night we stood outside the hut, catching the scent of the flowers and the more homely smell from the farm. To the east the horizon flickered incessantly with fire that changed from yellow to white and even green. The air shook with the din and every few seconds we saw flares curve upwards and hang in the sky, silhouetting the trees and making the twigs look as though they were covered with icing sugar. From time to time we heard a spasmodic burst of machine-gun fire and there was an occasional whisper of a shell and the distant crump of an explosion.

'Five miles away, they say,' Frank pointed out. 'Seems funny for a battle to be taking place that near, with us here and no sign of the war.'

The following morning, Frank was sent all the way back to St Omer to bring back an aeroplane to replace the one lost over enemy territory. 'Would have thought it'd have been much easier to fly him down in it,' Sykes said mildly.

I was allocated the machine which had damaged its undercarriage in a cross-wind landing and had now been repaired. In defiance of orders which forbade any form of decoration, it had *Daisy* painted round the observer's cockpit. It was heavy on the controls and flew one wing low – a relic of some earlier crash, I supposed – but at least it was mine.

'I'll get a chap to show you the lines this afternoon,' Sykes said lazily. 'He's due back any moment.'

The battle we'd seen the previous night turned out to be another British attempt to get up the slopes of Vimy Ridge before the winter came to stop all fighting. Sykes had flown above it, spotting for the artillery, and his machine still stood near the hangars, attended by mechanics, its fabric still torn, its neat varnish scarred. To watch him, though, you'd have thought he'd been on a picnic at which one of the guests had had a little too much to drink and grown rather rough.

I was desperately eager to get into the air because I was still terrified that the war would be over before I'd even seen it and, that afternoon, while Frank was still away, the observer who'd been allotted to me turned up. He was an enormous man with a ginger moustache called Wickitt who said he'd gone to war originally as a Corporal of Horse in the Blues and, before 1914, had even sat his mount in its box in Whitehall. When the war had broken out he'd been promoted with remarkable swiftness to sergeant-major as his contemporaries disappeared in the fighting and had then, on transfer to the Flying Corps, been granted a commission. He was a Yorkshireman who'd once been a small farmer until hard times had forced him into the Army, red-faced, broad of accent, cleverer than he allowed himself to seem, and not in the slightest bit condescending towards me. Daisy was the name of his girl friend and he'd been the observer when the machine had crashed.

'We'll fly towards Le Quesnoy,' he said. 'We can have a little look at a battery there I've noticed. Might as well make ourselves useful at the same time, and it'll give you the chance to find your way about.'

I began to wonder how he was going to jam himself into that narrow front cockpit and how, when he was in, *Daisy* would behave under his enormous weight. But he seemed to have everything worked out. He moved surprisingly easily in the cockpit and the aeroplane lifted off the ground without trouble.

Almost immediately, though, I began to hear an unusual noise from the front of the machine and my eyes flickered over the pressure gauges, thinking that the engine had developed a fault. Then it dawned on me that it was Wickitt singing. He went on singing, in fact, almost the whole time we were in the air, interrupting himself only to point things out to me or to give instructions.

He consulted the map frequently and shouted information, pointing downwards from time to time. It was difficult to hear over the engine and I was still a little bewildered by the newness of everything. Below me French peasants were still working in their fields and, though I saw the smoke of a train puffing westwards, I never saw a sign of troops.

Le Quesnoy looked a little battered, and I noticed that only the walls that ran east and west seemed to be unbroken, as though those that faced squarely towards the front were most vulnerable.

Just to the north I could see a canal, running south-east then swinging back west. I thought at first it was still in use, but I saw that for a long stretch through several locks it was overgrown with broken banks and was surrounded by scattered shell craters. Then I saw a trench running alongside it and I realised we'd reached the front line. Beyond here was occupied territory and I felt a nervous tremor of excitement at the thought that if I came down now I'd be a prisoner of war.

It gave me an odd committed feeling to look down on that fouled stretch of land that ran all the way from the sea to the Swiss frontier, the area that contained all the fighting, and had done ever since August, 1914, and was to do so until November, 1918. It looked torn, soured and battered, as though it had grown old in battle, with every building within its area smashed by shells, all its fields torn by fire, all its fences removed for firewood by the chilled troops. I'd heard so much about it, but it was vaguely disappointing. There seemed to be nothing left. It had been scoured clean, it seemed, and there was no sign of activity.

Wickitt's battery seemed to be well hidden and we turned north. East of Ypres, the ground looked even more desolate and emptier than ever. The soil was lighter where shells and digging had disturbed it, and farther to the north still the flooded fields shone in the grey light from the sky. There was little sign of that glory Frank and I had expected of the war, only dreariness and stalemate.

As I stared about me, I noticed Wickitt pointing upwards towards the south-west where the lowering sun hung in the sky like an amber ball.

'Always keep a look-out up there,' he shouted, the wind whipping at his moustache and scarf. 'That's where they come from. It's a new dodge they've got. Waiting in the sun.'

He consulted his map again, and I saw him make marks on it. Then, just at that moment, I heard a violent crack and felt the aeroplane lurch sickeningly, and my heart leapt to my mouth as I thought she was falling apart.

'Archibald, certainly not!' Wickitt shouted with a grin, quoting the words of the popular song, and I realised that anti-aircraft guns were shooting at us.

A puff of blue-grey smoke about the size of a haystack was drifting past just beyond the end of the wing and I saw holes appear in the fabric. The aircraft rocked twice more then Wickitt pointed down and indicated that I should make an S-turn and lose height. I did so at once and was delighted to see the next burst appear at the very spot where we should have been had we continued on the same course.

'Archie never hits anything,' Wickitt yelled. 'Just wastes ammunition. Better turn back.'

I banked sharply to the west, while Wickitt hung over the edge of his cockpit to stare downwards and make further marks on his map. By this time we were far enough from the lines to be able to enjoy the spectacle of the bursting shells without feeling in any danger.

'Best not to get too far over,' Wickitt shouted. 'Wind always blows from our end of the pitch and if you're not careful you find yourself blown *too* far. Makes it hard to get back.'

Now that we were out of harm's way, I felt tremendously brave and confident. Wickitt brought me back to earth quickly.

'Tourcoing's not far away,' he said. 'Fokkers have been operating from a field there.'

I looked round in alarm. I knew all about the deadly Fokker scouts which were cutting swathes into the ranks of outdated British reconnaissance machines like the BE2c. It was a rotary-engined aeroplane, with a single machine-gun mounted on the cowling to fire through the propeller. No one quite knew how this miracle was achieved and it was something that had been occupying British minds for some time. A Frenchman called Garros had been the first to try, fixing metal wedges to his propeller so that if the gun was fired, any bullets that hit it were deflected by the wedges, but it wasn't very satisfactory and he'd forced-landed and been captured soon afterwards – because of the strain put on his engine by his device, it was said. The Germans had turned his idea over to a Dutchman, Anthony Fokker, who was building aeroplanes for them, and he'd come up with something a great deal cleverer which stopped the gun when the blade of the propeller was in front of it. It seemed to work, too, and with it he'd given the Germans a weapon which was worrying the Flying Corps a great deal more than Sykes's casual indifference the day before would have suggested.

'Nothing to get excited about, though,' Wickitt was saying now. 'Some are better than others. You just have to get used to 'em.'

He pointed to the south again and grinned. He seemed eager to have another look at the battery near Le Quesnoy that was worrying him, and I swung the aeroplane in a wide circle over the lines again, then turned south towards Lille. This time when the anti-aircraft bursts came, I was ready for them and immediately lost height so that they next appeared above our heads and to the right. I began to feel splendidly experienced.

Lille, easily identifiable by the angular shape of its old fortifications, seemed empty of people. But I saw a shell burst among the houses and a cloud of red-brown dust rise in the air and blow off east like smoke from a chimney, and knew there must be troops down there.

I was still occupied in staring downwards when Wickitt suddenly stopped singing and shouted. His words were swept back to me and I lifted my head to catch sight of his wind-blown mouth. He was pointing upwards towards the south-west. I turned and stared, but I could see nothing and he pointed again, jabbing his finger furiously at the sky.

Then I saw a minute speck glittering in the sun, a thin line centred by a dot, and I realised it was an aeroplane. And it wasn't any aeroplane that I knew!

'Fokker!' I caught the word as it was blown back from Wickitt's mouth. 'Better get home! Quick!'

I swung the machine round, using all my strength and almost throwing Wickitt out in my alarm, and pushed the nose down. The air speed rose to sixty-five then seventy, and *Daisy* began to shake and shudder, and all round me the air was full of creaks and rattles.

Wickitt was manhandling the machine-gun from a position behind him to another on his left, and I glanced round in alarm. Things seemed to have come to a pretty pass if we were preparing to defend ourselves. I could still see that straight glittering line with its centred dot, hovering above us just to the south-west. It was almost across our path.

I swallowed, feeling my throat constrict. Just my luck, I thought bitterly, to come up against someone like Immelmann or Boelcke, one of the two great German pilots, on my first trip out.

Wickitt had turned in his seat now and was ready with the gun pointing out in the narrow arc between the propeller and the main spar where he could fire in safety without sawing off our own wing. I saw the Fokker change shape and slide towards our stern. The line grew thicker and the dot seemed to move along it, so that I realised the German pilot had turned aside and was probably at that moment preparing to attack us from behind. Wickitt's huge bulk obscured the view, but I kept *Daisy's* nose down and, with the wires whining in the wind and everything shuddering and rattling and twanging around me, thankfully saw the lines slide back beneath us so that we were safely over friendly territory.

Then I saw a great deal of activity on Wickitt's part. His hands moved rapidly as he put the gun at 'safe', and, struggling in the slipstream, yanked it from its socket and manhandled it to a position on the other side of the cockpit.

'Damned gun!' I could hear him swearing to himself, then abruptly, unexpectedly, he started firing and the racket almost made me jump out of my seat. I looked round to see where the Fokker was and Wickitt pointed, grinning, towards our tail.

'That's given him what for,' he said. 'Made him see we weren't asleep. He's off.'

Glancing round, I saw the Fokker again, a small neat white aeroplane with a single wing and a triangular construction of struts above the cockpit to support the wires that braced the wing-tips. It was dropping down below us now, quite close, in the direction of Tourcoing and I saw the pilot's head in a black leather helmet. I noticed he wasn't wearing a flying coat, and could even see the yellow collar of his tunic.

'Just up for a spin,' Wickitt said.

The German turned his head to look at us and I saw the sun glint momentarily on his goggles before he disappeared beneath the tail in a shallow engine-off dive. Wickitt smiled.

'Gone,' he said. 'Let's go home.'

When we landed, Wickitt examined the holes the anti-aircraft splinters had made in the wings.

'They're supposed to be fitting armour plate on some of the new machines,' he said. 'I reckon iron trousers would be better.'

Frank had returned from St Omer about half an hour before and proudly indicated the machine he'd flown back.

'Mine,' he said. 'Brand new. Well' – he gestured airily – 'it's been used a bit around St Omer. But it's *nearly* new.'

It didn't look all that new to me, but I didn't argue because he seemed so pleased with it.

'Flew it down without an observer,' he said. 'On my own. What have you been up to? Having a look round?'

He'd obviously decided that Wickitt and I had just been floating round above the aerodrome, getting the lie of the land.

'Oh, no,' I said, as airy as he'd been. 'We went for a look at the lines.'

Frank's jaw dropped and I saw Wickitt smile. 'The lines?' Frank said. 'You mean you've been up to the front?'

'Yes,' I said casually. 'Just to have a look at it, you know. Got shot at a bit.'

'Shot at?'

'Anti-aircraft fire. Splinters through the wings. That sort of thing.'

Wickitt was grinning broadly now.

'Good Lor',' Frank said, impressed enough even for me. 'What was it like?'

'Bit bad-tempered at times,' I said, quoting Sykes's magnificent understatement of the night before. 'Especially when the Fokker turned up.'

'Fokker!' I could see Frank was green with envy. 'You mean you were in a *fight*?'

'Yes. Terrific affair.'

Wickitt obviously decided we'd gone far enough and that it was time to let Frank off the hook.

He laughed, a booming friendly farmer's laugh, entirely without malice. 'Terrific?' he said. 'Don't you believe him, son. That German was just out taking the air.' He gave me a slap across the shoulder that felt as though I'd been hit by a swinging girder. 'One of these days, old son, we'll meet someone who's really spiteful and then you'd better look out. He wasn't even trying.'

'We'd have put up a good show, all the same,' I said stoutly. 'Even if he had been.'

Wickitt gave another great booming laugh. 'Think so?' he said. 'Me and Sykes once attacked a balloon in a BE. Of the two I reckon the balloon was p'r'aps the most dangerous.'

Chapter 7

Now that we both had our own aircraft, I saw surprisingly little of Frank. When I wasn't flying, he was; and when he wasn't I was, sitting behind the reassuring bulk of former Corporal of Horse Wickitt.

Wickitt taught me just what Geoffrey had meant when he'd told us we'd only just started to learn. Training and the real thing were poles apart, as he'd learned in the infantry, and I soon began to realise that, as a danger to the enemy, I was as menacing as a babe in arms.

'You've got to watch the sun,' he kept telling me. 'Always. Not just occasionally or when you feel bored or tired of looking at the altimeter. Always. Up there. Shove one thumb over your eye. It kills the glare and allows you to see close to it. And look down, too. For Huns. And when I say "look", I mean "look", not just "skate your eyes across it". It's blue and grey patching, isn't it? Well, that's how he paints his aeroplanes these days.'

Then he jabbed a thick finger at the tail of the machine. 'And keep one eye on that. On your rear end. On your *derrière*. All the time. Till your neck aches with turning your head. Because if trouble comes, it'll come fast, and that's where it'll come from.'

Between bursts of the latest music-hall hits he taught me how to deal with Archie – 'Ess,' he yelled. 'Ess like hell. Go into an S-turn and lose height. It puts 'em off' – and always to watch the wind so that we weren't caught too far beyond the German lines with it blowing against us.

'The speed *we* go,' he pointed out, 'it can bring us to a dead halt.'

Vimy Ridge had been fought and winter was near and preparations were now going forward for the big battles of the following year, and our duties often carried Frank and me in different directions. No one had thought yet of flying patrols of several aircraft, and I very soon discovered that for the purpose of active service, the BE was about as useless as it was possible to be.

'As a weapon of war,' Wickitt said, 'it's about as good as a bow and arrer. It ain't the magnificent modern machine they told you about in England. In fact, if you ask me, it's the aeroplane with everything in the wrong place.'

He was dead right, of course, as I soon found out. While *I* had a good enough view, Wickitt, who was supposed to do the observing, couldn't see a thing. In our defence, he could fire his gun in small arcs only in certain directions, and because of his lack of view, even the camera had to be operated by me while I flew the aeroplane one-handed.

Air fighting, fortunately, was still in its infancy and that first brush with the Fokker I'd had was roughly what normally passed for an aerial battle. It wasn't long since bombs had been hand grenades or simply canisters filled with petrol, and aeroplanes blundering on each other in the air had edged gingerly closer to enable their observers to fire at each other with rifles.

Eventually, a few aggressive pilots had tried taking automatic weapons up, but their engines had been so weak they'd found they couldn't climb with the extra weight, and as they'd have had to settle for leaving the observer behind to get within range, shooting had become almost impossible. Some aeroplanes still carried rifles, in fact, even in 1915, because with the infantry crying out for more and more automatic weapons, there was a shortage of them for the air, where they were rarely used because no one had yet learned much about deflection shooting and other such mysteries.

For the most part, when a German machine – usually a two-seater reconnaissance aeroplane like our own – was seen, we manoeuvred round each other, trying to bring our awkwardly mounted guns to bear in a skirmish that never looked like being anything else but indecisive. If the enemy pilot wasn't eager for a fight, it was very difficult, with our low speeds and clumsy manoeuvrability, to engage him. As often as not, such meetings ended with a friendly wave, and engine failure still accounted for most of the casualties on both sides.

Our duties consisted largely of what was known as contact patrols – aerial liaison between the troops and headquarters – and artillery observation. But since radio was heavy and clumsy, most messages from the ground to us were by means of flares or sheets of pegged-down cloth, and from us to the ground by means of weighted bags. Artillery observation consisted of circling over batteries watching for shell-bursts and Morse-ing simple letters to indicate whether the burst was on target, short or over, or waiting for the flash of enemy batteries and giving the pinpoint position to our own guns to knock it out. Only occasionally did we grow ambitious and decide to drop a bomb but, as this was usually more dangerous to us than it was to the enemy, for the most part we left well alone and did no more than toss an occasional grenade over the side.

Every job was done by the same machines because specialised types hadn't yet been thought of, though we'd heard that somewhere in the dim and distant shadows behind us things were stirring in the dark.

'Somebody at H.Q.'s bound to think of it one of these days,' Sykes said in his lazy way. 'Seems sensible. One aircraft. One job, what?'

'Why not?' Wickitt agreed. 'The Hun's always one jump ahead of us and *he's* thought of it.'

But only just. The *jagdstäffeln*, or pursuit squadrons, were *only just* appearing and, like us, for the most part the Germans operated their squadrons with slow reconnaissance machines with occasion-ally – if there was one handy, which normally there wasn't – a pursuit machine to frighten us off.

They had, however, produced the only real scout available so far and were beginning to group together small numbers of the dangerous little forward-firing Fokkers for trial.

When we discussed it in the mess or the hangars it appeared to be a situation that was likely to become dangerous.

'It seems to me,' I said, 'that it's a policy that could produce a lot of problems for us in the future.'

'Especially while we make it easier for 'em by doing all our flying beyond their lines,' Frank said.

'Surely it's the only policy worth having,' I said, loyal to my superior officers and their methods.

Frank was less naive. 'Can't say I like it, all the same,' he said.

'Of course not. We all dislike it – especially in bad weather. But at least we keep the initiative.'

Wickitt ended the argument with a point that was simply not debatable because it contained so much truth. 'And reconnaissance on your own side of the line don't produce much in the way of information, does it?' he said.

About this time I began a regular routine of patrolling, generally at dawn, on the watch for enemy aircraft. *Daisy* was an old machine and Frank and his observer, with their newer model, got the more exciting jobs deeper into enemy territory.

But labouring because of my age under the nick-name of Brat, which had been given to me by the fatherly Wickitt, I was still enthusiastic enough not to be bored by a job the older pilots refused to do. I had suddenly wakened up to the fact that flying was the most exciting thing a man could wish for. Up there in the clean crisp air of approaching winter, with the sky brighter than any groundling ever saw it, always changing, always full of colour, I began to find the first real confidence I'd ever had in myself in my life.

'*I* don't mind flying guard,' I said, 'so long as I can just fly.'

'Well, sooner you than me,' Frank said. 'It bores me stiff just floating round in space with nothing specific to do.'

The principal reason for the patrols was to stop German aircraft crossing our lines and, from the simple fact that I had the oldest machine and drew this least interesting job, evolved the fact that I later became the squadron's fighter pilot.

'Not that it means much in a BE,' I admitted.

'They only give you the duty because you've got the oldest machine and the oldest camera,' Frank grinned. 'And because you never bring back any results. Everything you ever do has to be done again by me or Sykes.'

I threw a boot at him, but I had to admit there was a lot of truth in what he said, and while the rest of the squadron quietly got on with the main job of reconnaissance and artillery observation, I was left to chase off marauding Germans.

But since *Daisy* was so slow and because it was virtually impossible for Wickitt to get a shot at anything from his position between the wings, we could hardly have been called dangerous. In the end, in fact, we settled for patrolling as high as we could get and just trying to look aggressive enough to discourage intruders.

The most we fired at, however, after that first exciting encounter with the Fokker, was the trenches – and that chiefly to make sure the gun was working – and once a kite balloon. As Wickitt said, the balloon was probably the more dangerous of the two because we could only fly past it through scattered anti-aircraft bursts and machine-gun fire, for Wickitt to use his gun. And since we had nothing in the way of incendiary ammunition, the only thing we could hope for was to drive it down to the ground, punctured.

Inevitably it came up again shortly afterwards and we returned faintly depressed by our lack of success – fortunately without damaged spars but with plenty of fabric flapping.

With the waning of the year, the weather was beginning to deteriorate into rain and high winds, but we flew whenever we could, through the ragged banks of cloud, climbing persistently through the murk until we reached the area above where the sun shone, to sit above a vast white plain that rolled like the thick wool on the back of an old sheep. But even when we saw an occasional enemy machine we hadn't the speed to close with it and do any damage. You could hardly chase much with a top speed of seventy miles an hour – or, in a steady dive, eighty-five, which made *Daisy* shake so much she was in danger of falling apart.

–

In November we had our second brush with the Germans. It was in the early morning and we'd already chased after one machine over Armentières, only to find it was another BE, and I was just turning away when I saw British anti-aircraft shells bursting a few miles away. Ours were white and the Germans' black, and I immediately suspected there must be a German aeroplane somewhere in the vicinity.

I could hear Wickitt giving 'They'll Never Believe Me' all he'd got in the front cockpit. He'd obviously not noticed the anti-aircraft bursts, and I pushed up my goggles and studied the sky where the puffs of smoke were now beginning to disperse.

After a while I spotted two aeroplanes astern of us and below, flying on the same course as us and just close enough for me to make out the black crosses on their wings. I banged at once on the fuselage behind Wickitt.

'Wickitt!'

As he turned, I pointed downwards.

'Huns!'

He grinned and sticking up a thumb to indicate he'd seen them, got busy with his gun.

The Germans were approaching closer now, clearly untroubled by our presence. In fact, instead of us attacking them, which was supposed to be the idea, they seemed to be about to attack us, and I could see the observer in the nearest machine, who was sitting behind the pilot, not in front like Wickitt, swinging his gun round towards me.

Wickitt's song came to an abrupt end and he came to life with a jerk, his big body moving in the confined space of his cockpit with amazing rapidity. It was difficult in the front seat, surrounded by wires and struts, not only to fire with safety but to fire at all. It was no wonder frustrated observers had been known to shoot off their own propellers in their attempts to get to grips with the Germans. There were four mountings round his cockpit and underneath the gun was a spike which could be slipped into them. From one, he could fire over the propeller and from others at his side he could fire through a small arc on either hand, while another allowed him – provided he was kneeling on his seat – to shoot towards the stern. Only the rear-firing position was much good, but, unfortunately, to use it we had to be flying away from the enemy, which was hardly in keeping with our role as a fighter.

At this particular moment Wickitt was struggling to get the gun, awkward in the slipstream of the propeller, into the rear socket, and with the Germans below us, firing upwards, even that wasn't much use.

'Turn! Turn!' he was yelling, making wild gestures to indicate the sort of tight bank *Daisy* could never have hoped to perform.

I heaved on the joystick and he peered over the side, waiting for the Germans to come into view, one arm still making frantic gestures.

'Tighter! Tighter!'

'I'll pull the wings off!'

By this time, however, he'd got his gun in position and the turn managed to give him a shot. But the Germans had already made off in a long dive which we couldn't hope to catch and Wickitt was fighting the gun back towards the forward mounting as I put the nose down to give chase.

It was pretty hopeless. Wickitt could only fire forward in an upwards direction and I would have had to dive directly beneath the Germans for him to get in a shot. In the end we settled for the mountings at the side of his cockpit and I kept swinging off course to give him a chance to pull the trigger. But with every turn away, of course, we lost ground and in the end we were much too far out of range for any further pursuit to be worth while.

When we landed, Wickitt started walking round the machine, frowning heavily and staring at it from all angles.

'Y'know, Brat,' he said, 'I reckon we need a hell of a lot of luck to do some damage with this blooming thing.'

I agreed with him, grinning at the expression on his face.

'Why don't they put the pilot in the front cockpit?' he went on. 'He's not important. He's only the driver. If they put the observer in the rear seat, they could fix the gun on a good revolving mounting and he'd be able to fire all round, even forward over the wings.'

'Still wouldn't make us very aggressive,' I pointed out.

'No. But that's what them Germans we met had done and they were shooting at us all the time and we couldn't even get near 'em.'

We discussed the matter with Frank over the bacon and eggs in the mess and he shrugged. 'According to Bill Sykes,' he said, 'they're doing everything they can to solve the problem. Guns on the wings. Guns sticking out of the side of the fuselage. Guns on the top plane...'

'And guns in me lady's chamber,' Wickitt growled. 'That won't help. We haven't got the engines to lift 'em.'

'Well, then, new methods of attack.'

'Everything, in fact, except the obvious,' Wickitt grumbled. 'Swopping the pilot and the observer round.'

–

I'd noticed from the moment we'd appeared that Frank had seemed excited and all through the conversation he'd hardly been able to contain some tremendous secret inside himself. As Wickitt rose and vanished, his eyes gleamed and I pounced on him.

'What's the matter with you?' I asked.

He looked startled, as though I'd caught him out in some misdemeanour. 'Me?' he said. 'Nothing.'

'Come off it. There's something going on. What is it? Got a letter from that girl of yours?'

He looked faintly guilty and leaned towards me. 'Keep it dark, won't you?'

'I don't know what it is yet.'

'I mean, I wouldn't want them to find out – Sykes, the C.O. That lot.'

'What have you done, for heaven's sake? Lost your observer over the line?'

He grinned. 'Not really. Nearly as bad, though, I suppose. I almost looped today.'

Though everyone was keen to say he'd done it, looping was heavily frowned on and my eyes widened. 'You did what?'

'I almost looped.'

'What do you mean? – you *almost* looped.'

He grinned sheepishly. 'Well, I was up alone and decided to try it.'

'But you didn't?'

'Well, no.'

'I should think not, in a BE.'

'It's been done,' he insisted. 'And I nearly did. I dived to get up speed and had just started to pull up when I got frightened silly, and changed it into a sort of half bank, half roll. I'm not sure what I did, in fact. I don't think I could do it again.'

'What was it like?'

'Awful.'

I felt envious for a moment – even though he hadn't quite made it – because my own flying always tended to be safe rather than spectacular. It was the ambition of every pilot to loop an aeroplane and we'd heard you *could* loop a BE if you had enough nerve. But thinking about it again, I couldn't quite see the point of the manoeuvre, because in a fight with a German I couldn't imagine any situation when it would be a good idea to turn the machine on its back. It seemed much more important to me to learn how to handle a spin if you found yourself in one, and none of us was really very sure about *that* yet.

'What's the point?' I asked.

'Point of what?' Frank asked.

'Looping.'

He seemed hurt by my indifference. 'Well,' he said, 'you can use it to change direction if you know how. They say Immelmann does a loop, and rolls off the top, so that he's changed direction.'

'You're not thinking of doing *that* in a BE, are you?' I asked.

'I might have to,' Frank said sternly. 'I think I'll have another go.'

'I should warn your observer first,' I grinned, 'or you might have to say goodbye to him rather abruptly.'

-

By this time the weather had really broken. The leaves had fallen and the trees were gaunt and empty. There was frost on the ground in the mornings and star-shaped patches of ice in the stiffened mud near the huts. The stubble crackled harshly underfoot and in the wind that lifted the leaves the canvas hangars billowed and collapsed and the aeroplanes rocked and shuddered at their moorings, their wires singing.

There was a succession of damp and misty days and little flying, and we stood with our hands in our pockets in the gloom of the hangars, staring at the sky and waiting for a break in the weather.

'Not what you'd call good visibility,' I said, shaking the drops of mist off my cap.

'We *might* be able to get up,' Frank observed hopefully, always eager to get on with the job.

'*You* might,' I said. '*I* couldn't.'

'You'd feel like a London bus going down Cheapside in a pea-souper,' Wickitt pointed out. 'To my mind, flying's best left alone when the weather's bad.'

'Birds fly in fog,' Frank said.

'I'm not a bird,' Wickitt observed.

'You don't look like one either,' I said, eyeing his bulk.

Frank was indignant at our lack of enthusiasm. 'One of these days,' he said loudly, 'there won't be a thing that a bird can do that a man in an aeroplane can't do, too. You see.'

Wickitt gave a loud hoot of laughter. 'You let me know, lad,' he said, 'when you see a bloke in a BE fast asleep on the branch of a tree in the dark with his head under his wing. That's one thing I'd go a long way to look at.'

But the bad weather continued and we grew restless with the need to do some damage to the enemy.

'I'd like to drop a bomb,' I said suddenly.

Wickitt stared at me as if I'd gone mad. 'What on earth for?' he demanded.

'People do,' I pointed out. 'There's a war on.'

'As if I hadn't noticed. What do you want to drop a bomb for? Why can't you let people live in peace? Besides, you've *dropped* a bomb. Once.'

'It was a long time ago,' I said. 'And in any case it was only a grenade we chucked over the side.'

He laughed, but the feeling had already become an obsession. We had to drop a bomb. The desire had been growing on me for some time and, badgered by me, Wickitt finally agreed.

'I'm a peace-loving chap meself,' he said, 'but you're young, I suppose. I expect you'll soon grow out of it.'

Bombs hadn't improved much and were still pretty primitive and we still knew nothing about aiming them as there weren't many and they weren't handed out without good reason, so we didn't get much practice. Our experience was limited to grenade-throwing, but this didn't seem technological enough to be called bomb-dropping.

The obsession grew. Photography and aerial spotting seemed a dreary occupation and our brushes with enemy machines seemed very brief and not very satisfying. I felt we weren't pushing the war hard enough. I was eager to carry it into the Germans' camp and in the end I took the flight sergeant armourer into my confidence.

He was much older than I was, with several children, and probably used to the hell-raising tactics of young pilots. He seemed to have decided to humour me.

'Leave it to me, sir,' he said.

The following morning he produced half a dozen stick grenades, the sort you fused by pulling a tape and then hurled at the enemy.

'How about *them,* sir?' he grinned. 'Scrounged 'em from the infantry.'

'They look like grenades to me. How do we drop them?'

'You just chuck 'em over the side, sir. Same as always.'

I frowned. 'I want to drop *bombs,*' I insisted, 'not chuck grenades. I've tried that.'

The flight sergeant glanced at Wickitt, but Wickitt shrugged and the flight sergeant went away to think about it a little more. The following day he called me into the hangar. He had rigged up a small rack and screwed it underneath the aeroplane by Wickitt's cockpit. It was filled with the grenades and there were a number of wires leading from it to Wickett's seat.

'I've fixed something up, sir,' he grinned, indicating it.

'Is that it?' I asked.

'Yes, sir.'

'They're still *grenades,*' I pointed out.

'Not now, sir.' The flight sergeant was a wise old bird and had probably learned to handle stubborn boys from his dealings with his own family. 'If I might quote: A grenade is an explosive article thrown *at* an enemy. A bomb's an explosive article dropped *on* an enemy.'

I don't know what he was quoting from but it sounded very official and I had to give him best. It seemed a fine point, nevertheless, especially when the same article was used for both operations. Still – I shrugged – it seemed to be either this or nothing.

'Will she fly with that stuck on underneath?' I asked.

'Of course, sir. All you have to do is pull one lot of wires to fuse the grenades and the other to let 'em go. If that's not bombing, I don't know what is. You have about five seconds before the bang.'

Wickitt was staring doubtfully at the contraption. Obviously he wasn't very keen.

'Wouldn't it have been better to fuse 'em and drop 'em with the same wire?' he asked.

The flight sergeant shook his head. 'Wouldn't work,' he said confidently.

I was a little disappointed, but I was growing more excited now. Wickitt was still not very keen.

He'd seen enough of the war not to be enthusiastic about it any more but he seemed willing to go along with me, if only to stop me doing myself some harm, and I took off full of good cheer and eager to do some damage on behalf of King and Country.

Just beyond the German lines we saw a battery of guns among some low brushwood. We spotted them first by their flashes and went down to investigate. Wickitt shook his head.

'No,' he shouted. 'Hand grenades won't do any harm against guns. You need high explosive for that.'

Disappointed, I searched a little further and eventually we found a battalion of troops on the march. I banged on the fuselage to draw Wickitt's attention.

'There,' I said, pointing. 'How about them?'

Wickitt grinned. 'They'll do,' he said.

We decided not to go low over the troops in case they guessed what we were up to and scattered, and instead floated above them as though we weren't in the slightest bit interested. When we were well and truly in position and suffering nothing more than occasional pot shots which came nowhere near us I signalled to Wickitt.

'Now!'

I saw him pull the first lot of wires and then the second, then his jaw dropped and his eyes grew large.

'They've not gone,' he screamed. 'And I've fused 'em!'

My heart dropped out at my boots. It seemed to me we had about four seconds to live, because when that half-dozen grenades went off there wouldn't be much left of *Dais* – or us either.

I began counting automatically, as though waiting a sentence of death. I felt like a condemned criminal standing on the trapdoor and waiting for the hangman to give the word to pull the lever.

'Two. Three.' My mind was numbly ticking off the seconds when I saw Wickitt jump up in his cockpit and come down with a thump on the floor. The shock seemed to shake the aircraft and almost immediately there was a flash from below and behind and a rippling crash as the six grenades went off. I heard pieces of metal whine past and one or two shot through the wings. A wire went with a twang and there was a series of ominous clicks against the engine, and it was only when I realised we were still flying that I became aware how lucky we'd been. The grenades had dropped away just in time and had exploded somewhere below the tail.

The wings and fuselage seemed to be in rags where all the splinters had passed through them and the machine didn't seem to be answering the controls properly. Fortunately, nothing vital seemed to have been damaged and neither Wickitt nor I seemed to have lost any portion of our anatomy. For a moment my nostrils were filled with the smell of explosive, then I hurriedly forgot the German battalion and concentrated on getting *Daisy* home before she fell to pieces.

I turned in a flat bank, expecting to see the wings drop off at any moment, but we made it and limped back to Illy at a speed only just above stalling, while I handled the controls as though they were made of icing sugar. Everybody was waiting as we landed. They'd all heard of our experiment and they ran forward as we touched down, strips of fabric flapping and wires trailing and a strange whirring sound coming from the engine. I don't know how much damage we'd done to the Germans but we'd certainly done plenty to *Daisy*.

Everyone hooted with laughter when they found out what had happened and Frank clung weakly to his observer, weeping with mirth.

'Oh, Lor',' he moaned. 'You'll be the death of me, Brat. You were always better at smashing up our own buses than the Germans'. There were two at Shoreham, I seem to remember.'

'A message's just arrived in the office,' someone else said. 'Have you heard? From the Kaiser. They've awarded you an Iron Cross for shooting down an English machine.'

Wickitt and I scowled at each other as they all yelled with laughter again, then it died abruptly as Sykes appeared.

'I think you'd better report to the C.O.'s office,' he said. He seemed to be trying to control *his* mirth, too.

The C.O., however, was in no two minds about what *he* thought. When we left his office a little later we were both shaken and white and not anxious to repeat the performance.

'Next time,' Wickitt said grimly, as we headed for the hut, 'we'll leave the war to run itself and not try to speed it up. It seems not only safer but pleasanter, too.'

It took quite a time to bring poor old *Daisy* up to scratch again, but the mechanics found it as much a joke as anyone else and forgave us the work we'd caused. Unfortunately, it coincided with the first spell of really good weather we'd had for some time and the C.O. didn't hesitate to point out how much more use *Daisy* would have been in the air than in the hangars; and made a point of repeating it when, just as *Daisy* came up to the start line once more, the weather broke again and we were back to the low cloud and drizzle.

'Makes you feel we're letting the side down a bit,' I said.

Wickitt grinned. 'Not on your life,' he said. 'As a matter of fact, I heard the C.O. laughing his socks off at it with Sykes when he didn't think anyone was listening.'

The information cheered me up a little, but the bad weather continued and Wickitt peered at the low skies gloomily.

'Any bloke who'd try to fly in that,' he said heavily, 'would worry rats.'

Since the collapse of the Loos offensive and the failure to capture the summit of Vimy Ridge we were all a little depressed. Somehow we'd hoped it might be the long awaited 'crack' that everyone had been predicting in the German line ever since August, 1914, but instead of a 'crack' it had turned out to be only a 'creak' and the line had stayed firmly in place.

'You wouldn't say we were overworked at the moment, would you?' Frank said, gazing at the clouds.

'Just thank God,' Wickitt suggested. 'And if we go up, we'll only have to turn back because of the conditions.'

We were a little dejected by the inefficiency of our machines because no one in authority seemed yet to have given much thought to the urgent problems of firing forward through the propeller.

'Seems to me the first essential in any aeroplane designed for war,' I pointed out, and Wickitt grinned.

'That's because you're a win-the-war-on-your-own merchant,' he said. 'But you have a point, son. The only objection is that these things we've got *weren't* designed for war. They were designed by the granny of some chap at headquarters for flying on the end of a string in Hyde Park on a still summer day. Shooting forward seems the first essential to *me*, too.'

'Especially when they constantly insist on a policy of aggressiveness,' Frank complained.

'You can hardly be aggressive when you're having to fly away from your target,' I said.

The highlights of our lives were the visits to the neighbouring town for an occasional meal and a bottle of wine. We were still young enough to imagine ourselves connoisseurs and we spent hours discussing the relative merits of burgundy and claret and pretending we knew all about them. Frank inevitably found a French girl to walk out with and because we worked together I found myself more and more in Wickitt's company.

From time to time, letters arrived from home, quiet, thoughtful letters from my mother which, despite the care with which they were worded, indicated between the lines the worry she felt. Since Geoffrey's death, Edith seemed to have slipped out of our orbit altogether. She was nursing in London, I gathered from the letters from Jane, who had undertaken to keep us supplied with news of the two families.

Your mother's got herself involved in good work for the wounded, she wrote, *and the Army's been to see your father. There's a danger he'll be in uniform soon, too, lecturing people on how Napoleon won his wars in the hope, I suppose, that someone'll eventually get an idea how to win* this *one.*

She was a good correspondent, writing in large round schoolgirl characters which, as she grew more absorbed in what she was saying, tailed off into a stronger and more forceful hand. She was frank and funny and was having lessons in type-writing in the hope of taking over the job of some man who'd gone into the Army. Edith, it seemed, was now virtually engaged to her doctor and, while I was shocked at first to think she could switch loyalties so quickly, I realised in the end that with wartime events moved much faster than normally and emotions were probably more intense, and that she was right to do what she had.

The tedium of winter went on, interrupted only by the disappearance over enemy territory of one of the pilots in our flight, a pleasant young man called Devereux whose nickname, because of a gift for playing the piano, was Tinkleplonk. His disappearance hit me harder because I was intimately involved in it.

'Long-range reconnaissance towards Douai,' the C.O. told us. 'The Germans are supposed to be building a new aerodrome there. We hear they're going to bring in the Fokkers.'

'Charming,' Wickitt commented heavily.

'We want every bit of information about them we can get,' the C.O. ended. 'Wickitt and Falconer will act as escort.'

The weather was bitterly cold and the sky full of ragged ugly clouds, and I wasn't looking forward very much to the trip. Sykes seemed to understand how I felt.

'Snow, shouldn't wonder,' he observed.

'Don't take any risks,' Frank advised. 'They don't supply shovels for scraping the wings clean in mid-air.'

When we had climbed through the layer of ragged clouds we found there was yet another layer above, heavy-bellied and the colour of lead, and, as Sykes had said, the weather had that harsh rawness that indicated snow. For once Wickitt wasn't singing.

We flew alongside Devereux for some time, careful not to lose sight of him because aeroplanes have a habit of appearing and disappearing rather abruptly in the air, and it wasn't hard to lose each other in bad weather. We stayed with him all the way to Cambrin, then a thin sleet began to fall from the clouds above, cutting off our view of him with what looked like tattered folds of waving grey cloth. We tried to edge nearer and, as the rain stopped again, we picked him up once more, but then it started to snow, which shut him off completely.

We were wet now and freezing cold and I saw that the glass of the air-speed indicator had frosted over so that I couldn't read it properly. The snow came more thickly, whirling about us and leaping away like a catherine wheel from the propeller. In a momentary break in the storm I saw a village below us, the bare black walls standing out against the snow as though the bones of the earth were showing through its thin flesh. By this time we'd completely lost sight of Devereux and when Wickitt turned to indicate our position on the map his face was like a mask. His nose and cheeks were patched with frozen flesh and there was ice along his eyelids. Moving my jaw, I realised I must look much the same. My hands were numb and my feet felt like dead lumps of stone and, now that I thought about it, I realised I was petrified with the cold.

I pointed at Wickitt's face and he nodded dumbly, trying to blink the ice off his eyelids.

'Bloody frozen,' he managed to shout.

'Me, too. Let's go down a bit.'

We had utterly lost Devereux by this time and there seemed to be little point in remaining so high. So I put the nose down to a glide, revving the engine from time to time to stop it freezing, and continued to head for Cambrin in the hope of spotting Devereux above us against the layer of cloud.

Wickitt was slapping his hands together now and stamping his heavy feet so hard to bring the circulation back, I felt sure he'd put one of them through the floor of the cockpit, so that I had visions of flying around with one of his great boots protruding beneath us. It would have gone badly with us if we'd been attacked at that moment because we were both a little stupefied with the cold, and Wickitt could never have handled the trigger of his gun. And by this time I was in agony myself as my frozen hands and feet thawed out. At least, however, when

Wickitt turned I saw that he was beginning to look more normal.

I cut the engine so we could talk.

'Any better?' I yelled.

'Only cold now,' Wickitt shouted back. 'Before I was solid ice.'

'No sign of Tinkleplonk.'

'Must have turned back.'

'Perhaps we'd better turn back, too.'

Wickitt bent over his gun again and I opened the throttle. But, as we turned over Douai, staring down at the torn ground, the snow unexpectedly cleared again and I found myself staring at an aeroplane. Where it had been a moment before I don't know but there it was in front of us, as large as life. It looked a little like an Aviatik, but the tail was different so it was either a new model or there'd been a little local adaptation made.

I came to life with a jerk, forgetting the temperature, and banged on the fuselage.

'Wickitt!'

Wickitt turned slowly, obviously still half frozen and miserable, and thinking I just wanted to discuss what to do next.

'There!' I jabbed a finger towards the German and I saw him come to life and reach for the gun.

The German was probably as miserable as we were, but he seemed slower than we did and we had a little advantage of height, so I put the nose down and, banking to avoid a cluster of anti-aircraft shells, headed towards where he hung in the sky in the watery light. Slowly we drew nearer, flying just to one side of him so that Wickitt could get in a burst or two, and I saw the German observer point towards us and swing his gun round. Faintly I heard him shooting but as nothing came near he didn't seem to be on target.

I jumped as Wickitt fired. The Lewis was a slow-firing gun and sounded a little like an old lady using false teeth, but Wickitt must have been shooting well because the German turned away quickly and began to dive for home.

Wickitt gave me the thumbs-up sign, but by this time I was beginning to grow worried. We'd been well over German territory when the chase had started and the wind was blowing, as it always did, from the west, carrying us deeper into occupied territory all the time. My eyes were all over the sky now because latest intelligence said the Germans had started to concentrate on producing Fokkers in large numbers and reports said there were more and more of them about. There might just be one or two on the new field at Douai already.

We were just above the German two-seater now, turning in a bank so that Wickitt could fire down at him without shooting off *Daisy's* wings, when I saw a flicker of movement in the sky by my shoulder that indicated an aeroplane. I pushed up my goggles quickly to get a better look at it and at once recognised the single line centred by a dot as a Fokker scout.

As he turned to move across our route home, without waiting to warn Wickitt I pulled *Daisy* out of the bank. I saw Wickitt let go of the gun and grab for a strut as he almost disappeared over the side. He gave me a pained look, as though I'd deliberately tried to get rid of him, and I jerked my hand upwards, gesturing frantically.

'Fokker!'

He stared at where I'd seen the Fokker and immediately started scrambling round in his seat to re-position the gun for firing over the propeller.

'Turn! Turn!' he shouted. 'I can't get the gun to bear!'

By this time, I had *Daisy's* nose facing west and we were going down in a steep dive, with the whole machine shaking and shuddering with its speed. Wickitt fired off a few bursts towards the Fokker to let him know we weren't asleep, then I heard the crack of bullets whipping past, and saw the Fokker sweep over our heads as he pulled out of the dive, so close I could hear the scream of his engine even above our own.

He was climbing now, behind us, up, up, and as I turned, I saw he was going to loop, and I felt foolish as I remembered what I'd said to Frank. *Here* was someone who could find a use for the manoeuvre! On top of the loop, however, just when I expected him to start down again, the machine rolled sideways so that it came out the right way up facing towards our tail to come down on us in another dive. It was Immelmann! It *had* to be Immelmann! That manoeuvre was supposed to be his particular trade mark.

I felt my heart thudding in my chest. Immelmann, like Boelcke, had a deadly reputation and was already said to have accounted for several British machines. But Wickitt was kneeling on the seat now, struggling to get the gun on the rear mounting to fire over the stern and, turning, straining my neck muscles to watch that deadly little machine, I found myself staring straight into the muzzle of the German's gun. Or so it seemed. All I could see of him was the circle of his rotary engine, the straight line of his wings, and the odd arrangement of undercarriage struts. He was near enough now for me to see the wires that braced the wings above the fuselage and the pilot's head, then I saw flashes just above the cowling and realised he was firing at us.

Fabric began to flap in the wings and I heard a bullet hit the top of the exhaust and go whining away over my head, then Wickitt was firing back, and a shadow passed overhead as the Fokker vanished.

Wickitt was cursing as he fought to get the gun on to its forward mounting once more. Glancing down, I saw the German had continued his dive beyond our nose and was turning below us to head east. He had swung in his seat to look back at us, and I saw he was only a young man with a small moustache. His goggles glinted in a pale light as his head lifted and I got a good view of his face before the machine banked away. I was certain it was Immelmann, and even though he was now heading east, apparently no longer interested in us, he was still too dangerous for me – especially in an elderly BE. I pushed the stick a little further forward, deciding to chance it, and with *Daisy* shaking as though her wings were coming off, we crossed the lines on our way home.

Frank was waiting by the hangars when we arrived and, as I jumped down, leaving Wickitt to disarm his gun and collect his maps he hurried towards me.

'Where's Tinkleplonk?' he asked.

'Isn't he back yet?'

'Not yet.'

'We lost him in a snowstorm early on. Conditions were frightful.'

By this time, Sykes had appeared with several other pilots. He listened to my story, frowning.

'Not your fault, of course,' he said. 'But I was up near Arras and I saw a BE being attacked by a Fokker. We're afraid it might be poor old Tinkle. He'd have been miles off course but none of the other BE squadrons had anybody up.'

The news took away all my pleasure at having escaped Immelmann.

'It probably *was* him,' I agreed. 'We very nearly became number two for the day.'

I indicated the torn fabric on my machine and they crowded round to stare. Wickitt was still in his place, staring over the fuselage at my cockpit. There was a bullet hole on each side of my seat that I'd not noticed, and the trajectory seemed to indicate that it was one of those the German had fired on his second pass at us. How it had traversed the cockpit without hitting me I couldn't imagine.

'You all right, Brat?' Wickitt asked.

'I feel all right.'

'Jump up and down,' he grinned. 'See if you rattle.'

His smile died as he learned of Devereux's disappearance, and we remained near the hangars for some time waiting for him to appear, staring towards the heavy sky in the east.

Time dragged on but there was no sign of that small dot that would become a missing machine, no faint buzzing sound to indicate that Devereux was on his way home. After a while people began to drift away from the hangars, until only Frank and I were left, staring eastwards with Devereux's mechanics.

It was the first time I'd waited by the hangars for an aeroplane that was never going to turn up. It was not to be the last.

Chapter 8

Christmas arrived, the second since people had said the war would be over by the end of the year, and there was still no sign of it finishing. Nineteen-sixteen came, a new year that also didn't seem to hold out much hope of a decision.

Devereux's death had left a gap in the squadron that was difficult to fill. He was an experienced man and his piano-playing was also greatly missed. Though Frank could coax a tune from the battered instrument in the mess, it was usually a laboured version of Lizst or Chopin that he'd learned at school, while Devereux had been able to play by ear and been invaluable for sing-songs.

The structure of the squadron had also changed a little by this time. It was a mixed affair now, with two flights of BE2cs and a flight of odds and ends, among them an Avro and two DH1s. The DH1s were probably among the only ones in France. A pusher fighter, with the observer sitting in the front seat behind a single Lewis, it was a heavy but manoeuvrable machine, though steady development of the tractor type of aeroplane was already making it obsolescent in every direction except one – it could fire forward and was therefore twice as useful as a tractor because it could fight.

Sykes had taken over the mixed flight and, with Devereux's disappearance, his replacement was given *Daisy*, and Wickitt and I were transferred to one of the DH1s.

'It's because no one else wants 'em,' Frank grinned. 'They've got no protection and they're too damn' cold.'

'Or else,' I said, 'it's because we always make a hash of the photographic jobs.'

'Not on your life,' Wickitt said stoutly. 'It's because we've always shown more aggressiveness than all the other crews put together.'

Wearing soft leather masks as a protection against the cold we'd feel in the exposed cockpits, we took to the DH1 like ducks to water. It was strong, faster and more manoeuvrable than *Daisy* and, above all, could fire at whatever we chose to chase.

'And if we're set on by a Fokker again,' Wickitt said grimly, 'this time, we'll be ready for him. I've got an extra Lewis I'm going to fit to the top wing so I can fire backwards without having to do a ballet dance round the cockpit to change the gun round.'

Though we didn't know it, we were already living through the development of the fighter aeroplane as a weapon. Until someone on our side of the lines discovered a means of making the gun fire through the propeller of the stronger and more streamlined tractors the DH1 was about the best we had. We still didn't belong to a fighter squadron, however, because they still didn't exist, though the authorities had at last seen the sense of the Germans' methods and were said to be assembling numbers of the improved version of the DH1 into groups in England with the idea of sending them to France to stop the inroads being made in our reconnaissance squadrons by the Fokkers. Rumour had it, in fact, that one or two single-seater DH2s were to be sent to squadrons, too, to be tried out by individual pilots.

We had no sooner got used to our new machine than we found ourselves using it as it was intended to be used. Our line patrols continued to drive away any German machines that might appear and one day over Armentières we finally woke up to the fact that we could be really dangerous.

There were so many aeroplanes about we hardly knew which one to investigate first, and we settled eventually for what seemed a fight over Ligny. A couple of Fokkers were worrying a group of FEs, which hung in the bright sunlit air in a tight box formation, their telescopic undercarriages dangling awkwardly like the legs of sick storks. They looked sturdy capable machines however, and the observers were climbing all over their cockpits to shoot. They were putting up such a good defence, in fact, they didn't need our help and finally drove the Fokkers off before we arrived.

Disappointed, we turned aside and found an Aviatik photographic two-seater over Rouge Croix heading towards our lines. At first it was hard to tell what it was, though we could see it wasn't a British or French machine, then I made out the silhouettes of his upper-wing crosses showing through the fabric. We were around nine thousand feet and he was a little higher, but for once we weren't very worried about that. We had a fast machine which climbed well, and we could fire forwards. I went straight for him – bull-headed, as Geoffrey always said I did.

The enemy observer, sitting in the rear cockpit, was wide awake. As I saw him swinging his machine-gun round towards us, I banged on the fuselage to tell Wickitt to fire. As his Lewis rattled, the Aviatik swung away and hurriedly headed back towards his own lines. Ten minutes later, as we turned away ourselves, he came back again, still above us and determined to do his job.

We made another attack, but as we climbed so did he, towards his own lines, and he managed to keep up above us all the time until the DH's controls grew sloppy and I saw Wickitt growing grey in the face with the cold. We had to give the German best again, and I turned towards our lines, losing height to allow Wickitt to recover.

Over Laventie, we waited, circling, fully expecting the Aviatik to appear again and, sure enough, eventually we saw it once more among the clouds. It was lower this time, busily photographing our trenches.

'Let's try it differently,' I shouted to Wickitt. 'Let's try it *their* way.'

I climbed as high as I could, keeping one eye all the time on the German, then it occurred to me to try Immelmann's tactics and sit up in the sun and wait our opportunity.

'Up there,' I shouted to Wickitt, pointing towards the glare. 'I'm going up there.'

I turned south-west again and found a position which, as nearly as I could judge, placed us right in the eye of the sun. The Aviatik went on happily photographing below us and when I judged that the crew had forgotten all about us I pushed the DH into a steep glide towards him.

The German didn't see us approaching and when I thought we were near enough I banged on the fuselage and Wickitt opened fire. The German observer's head came up at once and he shouted hastily to his pilot. Immediately the Aviatik dropped away in a steep bank and we overshot wildly and found ourselves a long way on the wrong side of him, frantically trying to turn to get back within reach while he calmly took pot shots at us with what seemed infuriating ease. I was angry that we'd missed, realising we'd made our attack far too soon, and I longed to be able to do an Immelmann turn to bring us back into position. Rumour had it, however, that the booms which held the fragile tail of the DH1 had a tendency to twist if it were too violently manoeuvred and, since we didn't wear parachutes, I wasn't anxious to be the one to find out the truth.

I heaved the DH round in as tight a bank as I dared and headed for the German again. By this time he was heading homewards in a steep glide, and we swung round him, Wickitt firing bursts as we worked our way behind.

'Go down,' he was yelling, pointing at the German. 'Lower! Lower!'

Taking up a position on his tail, we sat there at about two hundred yards' distance, pumping bullets into him but all with no apparent effect. This time I didn't try diving on to him as I'd done before, but throttled back a little and sat above him, allowing Wickitt to fire downwards.

The German pilot knew his business, however, and every time we approached any closer he turned back under us and as we struggled round to pick up our position again he bolted for home.

'Ess!' Wickitt kept yelling. 'Ess, for God's sake!'

It was a bit like a clumsy and not very clever terrier playing with a rather brainy rat, and with every move the rat drew nearer its hole.

By this time I was watching the sun myself, anxious not to repeat our little performance with Immelmann. But the sky appeared to be empty and, still watching my rear end, I fought the DH as near as I could get it to the German machine. From time to time the German observer fired back but they were not only less enthusiastic for a fight and more cautious than we were, but they were also a great deal more skilful. Their bullets kept coming close enough to us to force us to swing away, and several times, as I swerved in alarm, I almost threw Wickitt out of his seat.

We pursued the German all the way back past Lille, firing madly at him all the time until, in the end, just when I thought he ought to sink to the earth with the sheer weight of the lead I felt sure we'd pumped into him, Wickitt stopped firing.

'Shoot!' I screamed at him. 'For God's sake, shoot! What are you waiting for?'

He turned and indicated his gun and I realised he'd run out of ammunition.

'Oh, for God's sake,' I yelled furiously. 'Can't you throw something?'

I had wild ideas of flying directly above the German while Wickitt tried to drop an empty ammunition drum into his propeller or even trying to tear off his tail with my wheels, but I soon realised it was a hopeless idea, and by this time I saw he was descending rapidly so that we knew he was near his own aerodrome.

I looked round in alarm, fully expecting to see that lonely Fokker in the sky again because the story went that Immelmann had found a way of hovering without using his engine. Everyone who went near Lille seemed to report him sitting there waiting for a victim. I decided not to chance it and turned for home.

We were very despondent at our failure, but in the end we realised we had at least improved on our previous performances. If nothing else, we'd driven the German away instead of him driving *us* away, and we'd discovered that diving violently wasn't much good because it was too easy to overshoot and put yourself in a good position to be shot at.

'The idea seems to be to sit behind the German's tail doing whatever he does,' I said. 'That way, you can shoot at him whenever he stops manoeuvring and tries to fly straight and level. It's as easy as duck-shooting.'

'Except that out here the duck can shoot back,' Wickitt grinned. 'It becomes a little more difficult when you're trying to keep out of range of a gun yourself.'

We discussed the blind spots of German machines with Sykes, wondering which was the best way to approach.

'Ahead and above seems safest,' I said. 'In that position, the Hun observer can't bring his gun to bear.'

Wickitt pulled a face. 'Head-on attacks are over too quick,' he said. 'And we'll be going at him too fast, with his speed and our speed combined. It'll make shooting difficult.'

'How about under the wings, then? It's safe. No observer'll want to shoot his own wings off.'

'Then he's flying across our bow. He'll be out of range a bit quick and shooting at a chap crossing your front's always the hardest shot of all.'

I was just on the point of saying it was merely a deflection shot such as you'd use on duck flying across your front, but Wickitt had probably never shot duck flying across his front so I held my tongue, wishing for a moment that he was the pilot and I was the observer.

'Seems to me,' he said slowly, 'the obvious place's under the tail. Get your shot in before the pilot can swerve to give his observer a chance with the gun.'

Knowing how difficult we found it ourselves to communicate with each other in the air, we decided finally that a long dive from behind, so that the observer would be waiting for us to attack from above where he could shoot, would be the best. But then, instead of pulling up above him where he could hit us, we would continue the dive underneath and come up under his tail where he wouldn't be expecting us.

'Be a surprise for him, shouldn't wonder,' Sykes said cheerfully. 'Make him jump, what!'

–

We decided to give our theories a trial the next day and climbed up into a cold-looking grey sky, trying to decide whether we were nose-up or nose-down as we groped for the brighter light above the mist. It was harder than I'd imagined and there were moments when I had the sensation that the DH was poised ready to sideslip. I kept glancing nervously at the piece of string I'd tied to a strut: If it streamed back towards the tail, I knew we were flying as we should. If it streamed to one or the other side, we were in danger of losing control.

As we broke through, we found there was another layer of cloud above us and the sky was cold-looking and grey, shut off from both the sun and the earth, so that we had a dreary lonely feeling in the silvery light.

As we continued to climb, I spotted a grey-blue Aviatik just to the north over Bailleul heading south. I banged on the fuselage and pointed it out to Wickitt, and at once he swung his gun round and waited, tense as a terrier at a rat-hole.

Instead of heading direct for the Germans, which would only have frightened them away, I continued climbing away from them, hoping that if they saw us, they'd think we hadn't seen them. If we left it long enough, they might even grow careless. There was still more cunning than technical efficiency in air fighting.

Eventually, high in the cold sky, we saw the German below us, heading south still.

'He's either forgotten us or lost sight of us,' I said, cutting the engine to talk.

'He's decided we've gone home for sausage and sauerkraut,' Wickitt grinned. 'Let's go and remind him we haven't.'

I nodded and Wickitt hunched tensely behind his gun. My hands and feet were frozen by this time and I didn't like to think how Wickitt must have been feeling.

Putting the machine into a gentle dive, we went down in a slow curve until we were behind and above the Aviatik's tail, and almost at once I saw the German observer look up as he spotted us, and reach for his gun. I saw the weapon point in our direction as we approached, and a series of flashes, then we'd passed out of sight below and behind his tail and he had to stop firing for fear of hitting his own rear end. In the last moment before he disappeared from view behind the elevators I saw him swing in his cockpit and start gesturing at his pilot, but we'd already changed direction by this time and were pulling out of our dive. The German machine was directly above us now and I could see every rib and spar as the light shone through the fabric that covered them.

I saw Wickitt's gun barrel lift and heard its chatter, but by this time the German observer had got his message across and the Aviatik was turning. I heard bullets crack past us as the observer appeared again round the tail section and got in a long burst before I pulled the machine over in the bank and dropped below and round to come up again beneath him.

As I straightened up once more, Wickitt's gun clattered again, but by this time the German crew were working together well and the Aviatik swerved almost at once. By this time, too, he was heading downwards in a long slow glide homewards so that it was difficult to get below him and we had to content ourselves with simply chasing him. Then our chance came. We could see the German observer having trouble with his gun and I realised it was a clear opportunity to attack and, as I went in close, Wickitt gave them a long burst.

The German observer vanished from sight at once and the Aviatik went into a steep right-hand turn, dropping rapidly out of the sky. But I noticed now that there was a broken trail of oily blue smoke coming from his engine and I was convinced that we'd hit him. With the German observer clearly out of action, we came round again for another attack, and we saw the German's dive grow steeper and more erratic as he descended in tight spirals, still trailing that thin spasmodic cloud of blue smoke.

Convinced that he hadn't a chance to escape, we were intent on following him down when I suddenly remembered our rear end and glanced round sharply.

I saw the Fokker immediately, up there above us where it always seemed to be, waiting to snatch up his chance. He was already diving down on us and this time in alarm I saw there were two of them, not one. I banged furiously on the fuselage, shouting to Wickitt.

'Fokker!' I screamed.

He turned in a hurry, staring all round the sky. 'Where?'

I jabbed a hand behind us and he reached for the gun on the upper wing, while I swung the machine desperately towards home.

Grateful for a machine that was faster and more manoeuvrable than the old BE, I held the DH in as tight a bank as I dared and dived beneath the Fokkers, so that they'd overshoot. It was a manoeuvre we'd had tried on us more than once and it seemed a good one, and the two German machines hurtled past above us towards the east in a long dive.

By the grace of God, they were either short of fuel or just cold, and they made no attempt to pull out, but continued down in the direction of Lille, while we bolted for Illy as fast as we could go, shouting and laughing at each other and singing together all the way home, exhilarated by our escape and the belief that we had driven a German machine down.

–

'I reckon we did all right that time,' Wickitt grinned as we landed. 'I reckon we downed him all right.'

'If we didn't, we at least sent him off home with a sharp pain in the backside,' I said.

We had expected to be greeted like heroes, but Frank appeared with a long face. His observer, a young Canadian called Walsh, had been hit by anti-aircraft fire.

'He's just been carted off in the ambulance,' he said.

'Bad?' Wickitt asked.

'Splinter tore away part of his calf. He's in pain but he's pretty pleased with himself.'

'I should think so, too,' Wickitt said. 'A perfect Blighty. He can now retire from the war with the knowledge that he's done his bit and survived.'

There was still a crowd of officers round Frank's machine, gossiping excitedly and moving their hands to indicate the flight of aeroplanes, and Wickitt eyed them thoughtfully.

'This war's getting dangerous, Brat,' he said. 'People keep getting hurt.'

When eventually everybody got around to hearing our story of the fight with the Aviatik it seemed to have lost its punch and, compared with the loss of Walsh, even seemed unimportant. After all, we hadn't actually seen the German machine destroyed and it was known that there were some German planes which sent out a cloud of smoke from their exhausts when they opened the throttle, so there was no certainty even that we'd damaged it.

Wickitt and I felt certain we had, however.

'If nothing else,' Wickitt said, 'I hit the observer and that makes up for young Walsh.'

As we discussed it with Sykes, we began to feel we were getting the hang of air fighting. We were learning something new with every brush with the

Germans. Every fight gave us some new information, and experience was giving us confidence. We knew that eventually we should do exactly what we were supposed to do.

–

Two days later Wing demanded that the squadron lay on a bomb attack on a gun park at Cysoing. Every machine in the squadron that could fly was to go, together with those of our next-door neighbours, who were also flying BEs.

'Two one-hundred-pound bombs will be carried,' the C.O. announced.

'We'll never get off the ground,' Frank commented, and the C.O. smiled.

'We've thought of that,' he said. 'Guns will be left behind.'

Wickitt was to take Walsh's place with Frank and I was to fly as escort just above and, to make it possible for me to be of some use, Wickitt had his gun fixed to a rigid mount, just in front of my cockpit where, with difficulty, I could just manage to reach it. Changing drums would be difficult but not impossible, and the trigger was worked by a

Bowden cable carried back and mounted on the instrument panel.

'It looks jolly dangerous and not very certain,' Frank said with a grin. 'So just keep well away from me. I remember what you did to *Daisy* and those two buses at Shoreham.'

I flung my helmet at him and he dodged away, still laughing.

'I have a girl friend I hope to see again before long,' he said. 'And I'm not a win-the-war merchant like you.'

He was a little envious, all the same, and I noticed he was listening carefully as Wickitt explained his idea.

'If you want to aim the gun,' Wickitt said, 'you just aim the machine. Just like Immelmann and his Fokker.'

It seemed remarkably simple and I couldn't imagine why no one else had ever thought of the idea.

I took the machine up and fired several short bursts against the ground target. The gun shook a lot, but it seemed to work satisfactorily, and I was delighted. I was learning more about air fighting every day.

The rendezvous for the raid was over Seclin, and I arrived far behind the others. As a fighter and therefore unable to do a great deal of damage, I'd been last to take off and the machine ahead of me had crashed as it had rolled down the field. Its right wheel had dropped into a muddy rut so that it had canted over to dig in a wing-tip. As it slewed round with tearing fabric and splintering wood to collapse into wreckage, it was smack in my way. I'd had to swerve violently and go back for another try, and I was a long way back.

There were several machines circling above the lines when I arrived and as I climbed to join them I could see the bombs hanging beneath them. Towards the east a few more BEs straggled over the German lines, picking up their position along the railway line that ran to the gun park. It wasn't exactly a spectacular sight as there was no formation and the aeroplanes were following each other in ones and twos at different heights, surrounded by scattered bursts of Archie fire. Since they were all at different altitudes and all over the sky, the baffled gunners didn't seem to know which one to fire at.

Finding the target at last, the BEs flew round to the east so as to be able to approach into wind, a long straggle of ungainly machines fighting for position. Archie was still firing away, filling the sky with bursts of black smoke which, even if it didn't frighten anyone away, was certainly enough to put the observers off their aim.

I could see the gun park below us now, and the BEs were going down one after another to drop their bombs. I saw flashes and smoke, though whether any damage was done or not I couldn't tell. I saw a motor lorry on fire and a shed burning fiercely and I was longing to join in and even began to wish I'd still been flying a BE so I could drop a bomb, too.

Still watching, I swung towards the west, my eyes intermittently searching the sky, and there above me I saw a German two-seater gallantly coming to join the party.

He wasn't much faster than the BEs, but he was obviously intending to do what he could to stop them, and I climbed rapidly towards him. He hadn't seen me, but as soon as he did he swung away in alarm, then I saw the observer pointing and it dawned on me he was indicating that my front cockpit was empty.

Immediately, the German pilot straightened out and headed back for the BEs again. He'd obviously decided that I'd somehow lost my observer somewhere *en route* and was therefore unable to do him any damage, and he flew past me contemptuously, the observer banging away unsuccessfully at me as I scuttled past to try to get into a position where he couldn't fire back at me.

He didn't even bother to watch me go, and was now trying to get in a few shots at the unarmed BEs. He was having a great time, too, and the BEs, unable to fire back, were just beginning to scatter in alarm when I arrived back on the scene at full speed from behind, using the tactics Wickitt and I had worked out. Coming down on him in a shallow dive, I slipped beneath him, pulled up the nose and pressed the trigger in a long burst.

The Lewis gun jumped and shuddered on its stand, and I saw holes appear in the German plane's fuselage and tail. It swerved away violently, then I realised that the gun was firing all over the sky and I was in danger of shooting off my own wings. A pin the armourers had used to hold it in position had broken and the gun was swinging round on its stand so that I had to stop firing abruptly before I became my own first victim.

I was livid with rage, beating my fist on the fuselage in fury. It had seemed so much easier for me to aim the aeroplane than to wait for Wickitt, good as he was, to do the job for me, and I was convinced I'd had the German at my mercy. I swung away, cursing and shouting out loud at him, determined in my disappointment to put the armourers on a charge.

The German plane had sheered off now and was hovering out of gun range, its crew obviously frightened and staring balefully at the BEs. Still livid with rage, all I could do was make wild rushes at it that looked menacing but contained no element of danger whatsoever, so that it sheered off still further away. Fortunately, the Germans never realised that I was quite helpless and they eventually vanished east, and the BEs which had scattered like a cloud of starlings before a shotgun began to gather again to finish their job.

I was still furious and frustrated, but when I calmed down a little on the way home common sense told me that since we were still experimenting, it was hardly the fault of the armourers. I decided, all the same, that when I got back I'd get them to make a mounting for me that wouldn't fall apart next time I used the gun.

I had discovered a great truth about air fighting. It seemed to shine like a blinding light. I could see suddenly why Immelmann and Boelcke had become so dangerous and had downed so many of our machines. I wanted a fighter with a fixed gun firing forward so that I could do the flying and the shooting at the same time. It was so obviously the answer I was dying to get back to put my ideas to Sykes.

Chapter 9

I arrived back at Illy far behind everyone else and when I walked into the C.O.'s office everyone was talking at once. The bombing raid had been completely successful, it seemed, with only minor damage to the BEs. The usual roars of laughter went up when they heard what had happened to my gun.

Frank held one finger under his nose like the German Emperor's moustache and pretended to strut forward to give me a medal.

'Und to ze Herr Leutnant Falconer, he said,' 'who is ze best *flieger* ve haf, an Iron Cross first class. Ve all know how vell he directs his efforts to our cause.'

Spirits were high and they were all suggesting that they'd like to have another go at a lower altitude.

'How about you, Brat?' I was asked. 'Are you joining the fun this time?'

'Not he.' Frank grinned. 'He prefers to stay where he's got plenty of room. Up top. Where he can shoot himself down in comfort.'

I accepted the joking because I felt I'd made a great discovery and was no longer interested in bombing. Those times when I'd wished Wickitt could be the pilot and I could be the gunner were over now because I was both pilot *and* gunner and all I knew about duck-shooting could be put to some use. All I wanted was to try out my theories of a fixed-gun fighter.

The older men jeered a little in friendly fashion, laughing at my enthusiasm and my youth in the sort of jokes that Frank, who'd always looked older than his years, had escaped.

'Good old Brat,' they said. 'Out to win the war on his own.'

I smiled politely and said nothing, noticing that Sykes didn't laugh but listened carefully, nodding his head and making suggestions to improve my own ideas. The war might have been a bore for him, but he was shrewd and well aware that we weren't yet using our machines properly, and was always keen to try new methods.

That evening I went to the hangars and talked to the flight sergeant armourer. He agreed to fix up a better mount for the Lewis, and the following morning when it was finished I tried it out against the ground target. This time it seemed secure and satisfactory and I was itching to use it against the Germans.

'I'm glad I'm not one of these win-the-war-on-your-own merchants,' Frank said with a grin. 'They sometimes get killed.'

'I've had a few ideas,' I explained.

He laughed. 'The best idea *you* could have,' he said, 'would be one to finish the fighting so we could all go home.'

I brushed his sarcasm aside. 'I've discovered something,' I said excitedly. 'I've found out how to use a scout machine. You fire and fly at the same time. No observer. Nothing.'

'Not even any hands.' Frank laughed and shook his head. 'You can keep your ideas. I like an observer. He comforts me when I feel frightened. Especially old Wickitt. You'll not get *him* back in a hurry because they'd have an awful job shooting round someone as big as he is to hit *me*.'

A new observer had arrived to take Walsh's place by this time, but I felt I'd evolved a 'perfect fighter' and I said I didn't want him, thank you, and he continued to wander about the place like a lost soul waiting for someone to take him up.

I went on making my plans. I wasn't the only one making plans, I know now, because a lot of people were thinking at the time of the best way to put their aeroplanes to good use, but nothing was organised and everyone was working on his own. I tried to remember everything I could learn about my brushes with the Fokkers in the hope of finding out something about tactics, and began to read up all the notes we had about the machine itself in the belief that the more I knew about it the less dangerous it would become. Sykes was more than helpful and even gave me a couple of days off to go to St Omer in the tender to talk to the test pilots there.

'Some of 'em have actually flown one,' he said. 'We captured one some time ago. Heard its lethal qualities are a bit exaggerated.'

Frank watched me leave in envy. 'Now I know why you're experimenting, you rotten blighter,' he said. 'It's just to get a bit of extra leave, that's all.'

What Sykes had heard proved true. The stories of what the Fokker could do, I discovered, were largely legend. Granted the advantage of the gun firing through the propeller, it had proved no better than the Morane Biplane or the Parasol, but because

243

of the forward-firing gun the idea had spread that it was invincible, that it had qualities that made it impossible to destroy it. The tests had shown that these beliefs were mostly imaginary and that the Fokker's reputation had grown largely from the exaggerated stories of men who'd wisely decided, on seeing one, that it was safer to bolt for home first and ask questions afterwards, and had then had to explain away their flight. Their stories had been seized on by the newspapers with wild yarns about 'Fokker fodder' and 'the Fokker menace', but in my own few skirmishes I'd not found it anything very special in manoeuvre, except in the hands of Immelmann, who'd seemed able to do things with it no one else could do. I'd noticed, though, that even *his* turns hadn't been very violent and I wondered if perhaps the machine wasn't as sturdy as it ought to be and that the German pilots were afraid of it breaking up in mid-air.

Frank was cheerfully sarcastic about my efforts like everyone else.

'I expect you want your name in the V.C. Department of the *Daily Mail*,' he grinned.

Wickitt rushed to my defence. 'You leave Brat alone,' he said. 'He's doing all right. If we finally manage to win this blooming war, it'll be because somebody stopped to think about it.'

–

The second attack on the gun park took place three days later with seven undamaged machines and again I was detailed for escort duties. I flew happily off on my own, sitting above all the other aeroplanes, content to be solitary, preferring it, in fact. Much as I'd liked Wickitt, with his bulk and his unfailing good humour, I didn't enjoy being responsible for someone else in the air. The fact that I was operating the machine on my own gave me a tremendous feeling of freedom. If there were any risks to be taken in this new style of fighting I'd worked out, at least I was taking them alone.

This time, the BEs, encouraged by their earlier success, went down lower and with more confidence, and dropped their bombs successfully where they were intended to be dropped – right among the guns. I saw flashes and men running, and a horse galloping madly away, its saddle empty, a toy animal below the moving aeroplanes. As the BEs took their turn, lumbering into their descents, I circled above, my gaze against the bright sky, itching for someone to interfere.

Sure enough, they did, and I spotted the glitter of wings in the sun just as I expected to – the centre dot and straight line that indicated a Fokker.

Keeping one eye on the German, I placed myself squarely between him and the BEs, knowing that if he came down, he'd have to dodge me first. I had quite a job looking after seven BEs on my own, but I felt amazingly confident and sure of myself.

The Fokker had started its dive now, obviously not expecting much trouble from a solitary DH1 without an observer in the front seat. I just hoped that the Germans I'd attacked on the last raid hadn't talked to too many people and that their adventure wasn't too well known.

The Fokker was coming closer now in a steep glide, and as I turned to meet him, I heard his guns go and saw holes appear in the fabric of my wings. Then he swerved slightly towards the BEs and as he passed in front of me, presenting his underside to me, I pulled the trigger and saw the Lewis jumping on its mounting. Immediately the German's head turned towards me and his machine swerved violently as he banked away, losing height.

He was obviously startled at being shot at from an aeroplane where there didn't appear to be anyone to work the gun.

I'd fastened on his tail now and was following him down in a tight circle and as I saw him turn round to stare at me I knew it wasn't Immelmann. *He'd* seemed a younger man than this pilot, moustached, and with a confidence in the air that this pilot didn't show. I edged closer, convinced that I had him at my mercy, but as I pulled the trigger of the Lewis there was a single shot and then the gun stopped.

Furious, hammering with my gloved fist, I swung away to work over the jam, trying to free it. Getting the gun firing again, I turned back after the Fokker, but the pilot had obviously had enough and I saw him restart his engine in a cloud of blue smoke and vanish beneath me.

By the time I turned on to our course home, the BEs were heading west again in a strung-out line of ones and twos, far ahead of me, so I took up a position behind and above them trying to look dangerous. Despite my failure, I was not displeased with the events of the day. I felt more certain than ever that I'd found the answer to aerial fighting and only needed luck. I was so pleased with myself, in fact, that as we crossed the lines I finally, for the first and last time in my life, decided to try a loop.

It was a foolish thing to do because there'd been a few bullets through the wings and one might easily have hit some vital spar, but I still wasn't very experienced or had enough sense to realise this and decided to try my hand.

Glancing guiltily at the distant BEs to make sure no one was watching, I pushed the nose down until the speed reached ninety miles an hour. Imagining all the troops in the trenches below gazing upwards in awe at the intrepid aviator above risking his neck to amuse them, I took a deep breath as the speed built up and pulled back the stick. I was still very pleased with myself, but halfway up I did what Frank had done. With a shock I remembered all I'd heard about the DH's tail-booms not being as sound as they might be and changed my mind. Why I hadn't thought of this before I don't know – perhaps I was just feeling too sure of myself – but with a feeling of alarm I hurriedly pushed the stick forward again, and the load on the flying wires was transferred to the landing wires as the machine changed direction. The upward pressure was greater than I'd expected and I found myself nearly doing a nose dive out of the cockpit, and saw all my spare ammunition drums sail past my head and over the top plane. The next second I heard an almighty 'crunch' as they hit the propeller, which, of course, since the machine was a pusher, was revolving behind me.

The crash was followed by vibration that almost shook the machine apart and for a moment I felt it was actually crashing in pieces. With a thudding heart I realised that one of the blades of my propeller had vanished into flying matchwood, and I switched off at once and eased myself back into my seat, spitting out of my mouth the dust which the violent manoeuvre had lifted from the floor of the cockpit.

The DH wasn't answering the controls any more and I stared down in dry-mouthed terror, looking for somewhere to land. I was having to keep full right rudder to hold the machine straight now and I realised as I stared round me, looking for damage, that the lower right-hand tail-boom had been cut clean through by the flying propeller blade. The whole tail of the machine was sitting at the end of the other booms, twisted to one side and held in place only by a bracing wire.

The machine was flopping about the sky now like a winged duck and, sweating with fear, I picked a field as fast as I could to put it down. I fought her to tree-top level and lowered her to the grass as lightly as thistledown, terrified she'd suddenly fall apart on me and leave me sitting on nothing.

As soon as the machine lost flying speed, in fact, the tail section fell off and with wires twanging and breaking all round me, and accompanied by the sound of splintering wood and tearing fabric, the whole machine slid to a stop and gently subsided around me. I stepped out of the wreckage quite unharmed but feeling very foolish.

I returned to the squadron that evening, sadder and wiser after a long trek on foot, and Frank, who'd been growing worried at my absence, grabbed me and went into a wild relieved dance of joy. I hadn't the courage to tell him I'd won another 'victory' for the German Air Force. I'd never have lived it down.

Sykes received me in his office sympathetically. 'Heard you had a bit of a to-do with the DH1,' he said.

'A bit of a to-do' was putting it mildly, but it seemed wiser not to be too exact about what had happened and I told him I'd been hit when the Fokker had dived on me – which was true enough because he'd put one or two bullets through my wing-tips – and that, coming home, when I'd turned to meet another I'd seen approaching, the DH had begun to break up.

There had been no witnesses and I felt fairly safe in what I was saying. I don't know whether Sykes believed my story or not, because he'd been flying long enough to know everything that pilots got up to, but he accepted my explanation without comment and, as it happened, it didn't matter in the end.

That day he'd gone by car to St Omer and returned in a new single-seater DH2. Its design was similar to that of the DH1 but it was smaller and it had a bigger engine than the Renault which powered the DH1 and was said to be faster, particularly as it didn't have to carry a crew of two.

'I'll be flying it,' he announced. 'But you can fly my DH1 to St Omer tomorrow and pick up a second DH2 for yourself.'

I couldn't believe my luck.

'They're withdrawing the DH1s for home defence and the Middle East,' Sykes explained, 'and hoping to form scout squadrons of DH2s. They want us to try them out. Think you'd be interested?'

Would I be interested? I couldn't think why he'd chosen me for the honour, particularly as I was still a comparative newcomer to the squadron. But the aggressive role I'd gradually slipped into had made me less experienced as a reconnaissance pilot and artillery spotter, so it was natural, I supposed, that I should get the job.

'Like the way you go headfirst for 'em, too,' Sykes said. 'Think that's what's needed. And since you don't appear to have a machine at the moment, you're the obvious choice. Been doing rather well lately.'

The DH2 was one of the cleanest and best-looking of the pusher designs, although I found the cockpit cold because it was well forward of the engine and I received no protection at all and no warmth. It had a single Lewis fitted in a trough in the upper coaming of the nacelle, where it was easy to clear stoppages, and, because it was entirely built of wood except for the steel tail-booms, it was light and manoeuvrable. The performance was brisk and sensitive, but it required careful handling because the engine torque had a tendency to throw it into a spin.

'Still,' the instructor said as he handed it over, 'you know what to do if that happens.'

I didn't, as a matter of fact, because no one had ever officially told me and I'd never experienced one. I fished gently.

'Oh, of course!' I said. 'Is it different from the DH1?'

'No, just the same,' he said. 'Just cross your controls, full opposite rudder and stick forward, but be ready to stop her going the other way. After that you just pull out of the dive. Still, you know all that...'

'Yes,' I said, gratefully storing away the information. 'I know all that. Does she go into them easily?'

He grinned. 'Just trying losing speed,' he said.

I decided I *would* try, and get this business of spinning mastered once and for all.

The instructor was climbing out now. 'Don't strain the motor,' he concluded. 'The cylinders have a habit of parting company with the crankcase. Makes rather a mess.'

'Yes,' I said firmly. 'I'll watch that.'

Flying back from St Omer, I climbed to seven thousand feet and pulled back the throttle. As I lifted the nose, the machine lost speed, and started a left-hand spiral and began to feel like a flying brick. I saw the ground turning in front of me and saw the same field swing round in front of my eyes two or three times before I came out of the trance and decided to do something about it. I pushed the stick forward and kicked the rudder in the opposite direction and the machine came out of the spin with a jerk that almost sent it in the opposite turn. Levelling off, I was so exhilarated I did it twice more until I knew exactly what I was doing.

I was delighted with myself. I had spun an aeroplane deliberately and survived. I felt like Cortez looking for the first time at the Pacific. This was better than a loop.

Frank was envious when I got back, but only because more by luck than judgment I'd acquired a brand-new machine. He had no particular wish to fly the DH1 because he'd heard rumours that it was a death trap, and he was quite happy with Wickitt as his observer and more than satisfied to work with him as a team.

'I'm no lone wolf,' he said, 'and old Wickitt gives me confidence. Pity he's such a rotten singer.'

He handed me a letter. It was from Jane. It was some time since I'd heard from her and it came as a surprise to realise that people were actually still living in peace at the other side of the Channel. I'd heard reports of Zeppelins dropping bombs on London but I couldn't imagine the flat Norfolk marshes ravaged by warfare. They were too sleepy and things always moved far too slowly for that.

Edith got married last week, she wrote. *She'll still go on working, of course, because her husband's going to a hospital in France, so it doesn't make much difference really. She seems very happy, and I'm glad of that because I think it was worse for her when Geoffrey was killed than any of us realised. I hope I look as beautiful when I get married. We've kept all the photographs and I'll show them to you when you come on leave – if you ever come on leave! And if you can be bothered to walk over to see me!*

Up to that moment I hadn't really ever thought about leave. Other men had gone home and returned, but, somehow, when I'd arrived in France, going home again had never entered my mind. I'd slipped into a routine and accepted that it was to be my life for ever after, but, now that Jane had mentioned it, I began to grow homesick for the fields and dykes and trees I knew so well. I suddenly longed to be in a boat on Wroxham Broad, waiting in the reeds towards Coltishall for the duck to come over; longed to see the golden walls of Norwich and the high grey skies above the marshes, and hear the lap of water among the reeds. And curiously, too, I found myself looking forward to seeing Jane again.

I wrote back at once, asking her to pass on my congratulations to Edith and telling her that I was just about due for leave and, when I came, how about a day in the boat? It gave me a surprising satisfaction to write to her and I pulled her leg a little, telling her to wait for me before she got herself hitched up to anyone else.

Having written to Jane, I now found I was waiting for leave in a way that had never crossed my mind before.

'We must be about due,' I said to Frank.

'Not half we aren't,' he agreed. 'And I'm beginning to feel like painting London red.'

'Like that time when we first got into the Flying Corps!'

'Only this time it'll be better. How about making a few discreet enquiries in the squadron office? They can only chuck us out.'

In fact they were much more receptive than we'd expected.

'You're due in three weeks' time,' we were told. 'As soon as the older hands are back.'

'Any chance of going together?' I asked.

'Don't see why not. They're anxious for us to fit everyone in before the spring offensives start!'

Frank and I exchanged glances. 'When will that be?' Frank asked.

'When the weather improves. They have to keep the generals happy.'

Nobody liked the sound of offensives. They had a habit of being dangerous. But so far there was little sign of the latest and I was delighted with my role as a fighter pilot and with my new machine. I took it up and tried it out at all altitudes to find out what it would do, turning it, spinning it, doing everything I imagined I might have to do with it in the event of meeting with a German, diving on the ground target and making dummy attacks on the BEs from every possible angle as they passed me in the air.

Rather to my surprise, Jane replied at once to my letter to say she'd finished her training and could now use a typewriter as well as anyone and was expecting to get a job in Norwich, but that she'd wait until I'd had leave so there'd be someone at home to talk to when I arrived, because everyone else our age seemed to have vanished.

Things have changed since you went, she said. *You'll need someone to hold your hand.*

The letter ended with the suggestion that I should bring Frank along, too, and I was curiously pleased at the casual way he was mentioned, as though he weren't very important to her.

Sykes had ideas of us flying the DH2s together, as a pair, doing damage to the Germans while mutually protecting each other from attack.

'It's what Immelmann and Boelcke are supposed to be doing,' he explained in his bored way. 'Found two machines are better than one. More manoeuvrable than a bigger number and two pilots who're used to each other can work well together. See what you can think up.'

Working together seemed to make sense.

'If two scouts attack a two-seater together from opposite sides,' I pointed out, 'the observer can't shoot at both of us at the same time, so we *ought* to have more success. The chances are that he won't even hit either of us. While one of us is firing at him, the other can approach from the other side while he's busy. We might be lucky and, if nothing else, it ought to put him off his aim.'

Sykes nodded. 'Worth a try,' he agreed.

To test my theories, Frank went up with Wickitt, and Sykes and I practised flying together against them. While we attacked from opposite sides at the same time, Wickitt swung his gun about, trying to cover us both at once. When we'd all landed we gathered in the mess and over a drink tried to decide what we'd done wrong, exchanged ideas and viewpoints, and tried to make up our minds which was the best way to tackle a German two-seater.

'You can't lump 'em all together,' Frank said. 'You can't go at 'em all the same way because they're all different. Some are fast. Some turn better. They've all got to be attacked differently.'

Though we didn't know it, we were working out fighter tactics for the future before anyone but the Germans had ever really thought about such things.

'There's another thing I've noticed,' I said. 'When the Huns come up in the early morning they stand out against the sky. I've seen 'em. Lit up by the sun, with the sky all golden behind.'

'Oh Gawd,' Wickitt said. 'Listen to the poet in him coming out.'

I ignored the jeer, though flying had really got into my blood by this time and the sight of a small glowing machine, on fire with the early sun against a sky just turning from lemon-pink to steely blue, always stirred me with its beauty.

'Why not sit low down?' I went on. 'In the shadows where the sun hasn't reached. You can see 'em clear as crystal against the light from there and they can't see you. Just as they can see us in the west in the evening when the sun's going down and we can't see them.'

'We might try our luck,' Sykes decided. 'How about tomorrow?'

'Sounds fine.'

As it happened it never came to anything and all our practices and all our discussions came to nothing in the end.

Sykes had been having trouble with his engine for some time and that evening he took his machine up in the last of the daylight to make sure it was running well for the following morning.

We watched the DH head towards the line, a flimsy fragile thing with the long tail-booms catching the late sun, then we turned away to our own duties. Frank and Wickitt vanished to the mess, and I went to watch the mechanics preparing my machine.

After a while I noticed that Sykes's mechanics were outside the hangar anxiously studying the sky and, glancing at my watch, I realised he was late returning.

After a few more minutes Wickitt appeared, then Frank, then the C.O. with a few other officers.

'Sykes's late,' the C.O. said.

We checked times and minutes slipped by as we waited. Sykes had already overstayed his time aloft and we were beginning to grow worried when we heard the faint buzz of an engine towards the east.

'That's him,' Frank said, and the mechanics came out of the hangars to wait.

The DH2 came over the trees in the amber light of evening and I knew at once that something had happened because it was flying left wing low and, as it came over our heads, I saw wires trailing and heard the motor making a strange whirring noise.

More men appeared by the hangars and we watched as Sykes manoeuvred awkwardly over the end of the field for his final approach. He seemed to be having difficulty because that left wing kept dropping and we realised he must have bumped into a German and was either wounded or had suffered damage to his machine.

The DH2 came in, still flying awkwardly, narrowly missed the trees, and banged down hard. It bounced, then the left wing dropped and touched. I saw pieces fly off as the machine slewed round and a wheel bounced into the air, and we heard a sound like a matchbox being crushed, strangely weak and small. Then the machine was sliding across the ground, cutting a great gash in the turf, fragments whirring into the air as it came to a stop.

We were all running across the field as fast as we could go but, to our surprise, Sykes climbed from the machine on his own as we arrived. His face was pale and strained under the cordite that marked his chin but otherwise he looked all right. But even as we approached, a spasm of pain crossed his features and he sat down abruptly, tried to smile, and flopped backwards on the grass.

Then we saw that the back of his coat was covered with blood and as the ambulance screamed to a stop, we lifted his head and pulled off his helmet to expose his flattened stiffening hair.

He'd bumped into a two-seater on its own over Lille and, thinking it was easy meat, had attacked. But again the Germans were thinking ahead of us and were trying a new trick. It had been a decoy and Sykes had been pounced on out of the sun by a Fokker.

'Bad-tempered type,' he said faintly, as we lifted him into the ambulance. 'Immelmann, shouldn't wonder.'

Chapter 10

The following morning at dawn I was over Lille waiting for a sight of that hovering Fokker which always seemed to be waiting there.

Sykes wasn't dead, but they'd rushed him off to hospital with a bullet in the back of his neck. Despite the loss of blood and once fading into unconsciousness, he'd managed to get his machine back and, despite the spectacular nature of his crash, it wasn't a complete write-off.

I was so angry at his being hurt I went off alone to be up above Lille before anyone else was in the air, in the hope of catching Immelmann unawares. It was little more than a gesture because the sky's immense, and I never saw a thing.

I'd gone up with wild thoughts of vengeance in my mind and achieved nothing, and I was much calmer when I landed again at Illy. It had been bitterly cold and the absence of activity had given me time to do some serious thinking about how to tackle Germans now that I no longer had Sykes to help.

The major said that when Sykes's machine was repaired, Frank was to have it. He seemed to like to encourage the younger members of the squadron with the new fast single-seaters.

'The older chaps are better at the run-of-the-mill stuff,' he said. 'They've got the calmer temperament for reconnaissance and artillery spotting and bombing. I think they've also got more sense. But you young chaps are more hot-blooded about this fighting business and, I think, properly trained and eventually with the right machines, it's you who'll be doing all the damage.'

I didn't realise it, but it was a prophecy.

Now that his chance to fly the DH2 had come, Frank switched loyalties overnight and was itching to get at it.

'Changed your tune a bit, haven't you?' I grinned.

He shrugged. 'Can't let you reap *all* the glory,' he pointed out.

I showed him the ropes with it, together with one or two other younger pilots.

'Got to have someone to do the work when we go on leave,' I said.

Whenever one of the BEs went up on one of the long reconnaissances I escorted it as far as I could or met it on the way back to see it safely home at a time when its fuel was running low and the westerly wind was reducing its speed to a minimum, and I particularly enjoyed working with Frank and Wickitt because, in our experimental flights with Sykes, we'd developed a series of signals so that we each knew what the other was going to do. These developed into still more basic ones which indicated that we were hungry, thirsty, or simply bored.

Occasionally, I saw a German machine and gave chase but without any success. Many times I was in a good position but I never seemed to hit anything as I manoeuvred in to a range of a hundred yards, a distance which, to me, seemed remarkably dangerous, especially when I was looking straight down the muzzle of the observer's machine-gun. I grew frustrated with my lack of success and Frank suggested that I drop a note at Douai.

'Arrange to settle it with fists on neutral territory at a distance of two paces,' he suggested. 'You'll have a better chance of hitting 'em.'

I was growing depressed again with my non-success, and it became worse when Jane wrote to ask if I'd shot down any Germans yet.

'*Other people have*,' she said.

'I've never met any,' I pointed out to Frank. 'She's been reading the newspapers again. They're always full of stories about "death dives" and "intrepid birdmen".'

'And full of pictures of aeroplanes which might have been flown in 1913,' Frank laughed, 'but certainly aren't now.'

Leave was drawing closer now and Frank and I were hopping with excitement.

'Had a letter from that girl I met when I was on leave from Shoreham,' Frank said. 'Says she's looking forward to seeing me home. Come to that,' he added. 'So am I.'

Since Edith had grown beyond my reach, I'd never had a girl, but I supposed Jane would fill the gap until someone better came along. She was always good at doing the things I liked, such as sailing and walking, and even seemed genuinely interested in flying.

'How about you?' Frank asked. 'Going to see the beauteous Jane?'

'I expect so,' I said. 'Pity she's so young.'

Frank stared at me sorrowfully. 'Oh, come off it, Methuselah,' he said. 'I hadn't noticed *you* were all that old yourself.'

Our kit was already packed for the off and we only had to wait for two other men to return before we could go, and we were trying to pick all the easy jobs so that an engine failure wouldn't force us down behind the German lines before the great day.

'Be just our luck for something like that to happen,' Frank said.

He was nearer the truth than he knew.

Two days before we were due to be driven by tender to the railhead to catch the train to Calais and the boat to England, the C.O. called us all in the mess.

'There's to be a raid on Avelghelm,' he said. 'It's a railway junction and an important one.'

'How many machines, sir?' Frank asked uneasily.

The C.O. looked at him and smiled sympathetically. '*All* machines, I'm afraid,' he said. 'However, I promise that all leave men shall go as soon as it's done. There'll be the usual hundred-pound bombs.'

'What filthy luck,' Frank said as we were dismissed. 'You'd have thought they might have got some other mob to do the job for once.'

Wickitt grinned. 'How about the chaps in *that* mob who're going on leave?' he asked. He imitated Frank's voice. '"You'd think they'd have got some other mob to do the job, wouldn't you?"'

Frank threw his cap at him, red-faced and angry, and Wickitt dodged away, laughing.

Frank remained gloomy and not his usual cheerful self. For a while I was irritated by his sharpness with me, then I realised that he was tired and in need of leave and made up my mind to keep a special eye on him.

I had never forgotten how he'd rallied round when Geoffrey had been killed, how he'd been there just when he was needed, with just what was needed. Despite his light-hearted attitude to life, he was a sensitive, intelligent, thoughtful individual and, without him, breaking the news to Edith and to my parents would have been a great deal harder.

But there was no dodging the raid. It was the gun park at Cysoing all over again, except that Avelghelm was about forty miles to the north-east and a long dog's-leg course had been plotted to avoid trouble. I was to fly as escort, but, as we had a lot of enemy territory to cover, I was to be assisted this time by a couple of single-seater Moranes from a squadron at the other side of the field, with the wedge-like bullet-deflectors fitted to their propellers so they could fire forward. No one relished the trip because the weather was indifferent and the wind was blowing strongly – as usual in the wrong direction.

'Never mind,' Frank said cheerfully, optimistic again now. 'By the time we come back, we'll be due for leave, and all we'll have to do is wash, spit on our shoes and give 'em a rub, and away we go.'

'And just behave yourselves, too, when you get home,' Wickitt added solemnly. 'Young lads your age oughta stick close to their mums, and not get up to mischief.'

The wind blew gustily on the morning of the raid, carrying before it ragged banners of cloud. It wasn't exactly encouraging weather, but, at least, if anything tried to make trouble there were always clouds to hide in. There was a darkness in the sky I didn't like, though, a stormy look that seemed to indicate worse weather to come.

'I don't like that damned sky,' I said to Wickitt.

He glanced sharply at me, fatherly and considerate. 'Why not?'

'Funny colour,' I said.

He stared at it. 'Looks normal enough to me.'

'It doesn't to me.'

He looked again at me, concerned. 'You feeling all right?' he asked.

'Bit shivery,' I said. 'Perhaps I've got a cold coming on.' I managed a grin. 'Sheer nerves really, I think. I'd feel better about it if I'd had a spot of leave.'

He nodded gravely. 'Well, there's something in that,' he agreed. 'You and young Frank have been in the air ever since you arrived in France and flying's a tiring business when you're at it all day and every day.'

All the previous night, the mechanics had been busy over the machines and they stood now in a long line like a lot of fragile white dragonflies. The little DH2 at the end of the line looked the most fragile of the lot with its tail-booms and the absence of a covered fuselage, but I felt happier with it than I ever had with a BE. At least, I often thought, if someone attacked me, I could hit back.

The C.O. came out of the office, followed by the flight commanders, and Frank and Wickitt and the other pilots gathered round them to hear last-minute instructions. Pencil scratchings about targets were entered into notebooks and maps were carefully marked. I waited on one side because this didn't concern me. All I had to do was stick with the others.

'All right!' the major's voice came to me over the muttering. 'Take-off in five minutes.'

Frank came past me. His face was cheerful, but he looked pale and strained.

'Take care of yourself, Brat,' he said. 'Don't go shooting yourself down, will you?'

'Not likely. Not this time.'

'Got a date in London, remember. Paint the town red.'

'That's the stuff. I'll be back first. I fly a machine that can shift a bit, you know. I'll have your stuff waiting ready for you to jump straight in the tender for the railhead.'

He slapped my shoulder and moved after the other pilots to his machine, walking awkwardly in his clumsy flying boots and looking like a bear in his leather coat and helmet and wrapping of scarf and gloves. I climbed into the cockpit of the DH2, making sure my revolver and map case and Very pistol were handy. I also had a small bag of tools which I carried because I was determined, if I had to land on the other side of the line, to have a go at repairing the engine and taking off again, a toothbrush and razor for if I didn't manage it, and a compass in case I got a chance to make my way back to the lines on foot.

The clouds were racing over the field now and I could see the bare poplars at the end bending in the wind. The C.O. raised his hand and, as the mechanics kicked the chocks firmly under the wheels and reached for the propellers, I could hear shouts up and down the line.

'Switch off?'

'Switch off.'

'Contact?'

'Contact.'

My mechanic laid his weight against the propeller, swinging his leg, and I felt the engine fire and the machine begin to shudder on its wheels. Waiting patiently in the little pulpit-like cockpit behind the gun while the engines warmed up, I listened to the drumming of the wings and the vibrating of the wires as I tested the magnetos. At last the C.O. raised his arm and the first BE began to jolt and rock down the field, gathering speed as it did so.

When they were all off, I opened the throttle and signalled to the mechanics, and felt the rumble as the DH began to move. After a while, as the speed increased, the rattling stopped and I was flying, climbing into position behind the others with the two Moranes who were to give additional support.

With the wind behind us, we seemed to hurtle towards the lines. There were heavy clouds above us, keeping out the light, and broken clouds below us, giving us only occasional glimpses of the land.

I cocked the gun and cleared it with a short burst, and we were nearing ten thousand feet, approaching Ledeghem from the south-west, when I saw a couple of specks to the south near Menin.

'Here we go,' I thought. 'This is where the fun starts.'

My hands moved confidently over the switches and throttle and the cocking handle of the gun, and I felt the nervous emptiness of excitement. 'At least,' I thought, 'there are three of us this time. We ought to put up a good show.'

Then I realised that the pilots of the Moranes had seen the specks. They were waving to each other and, to my disgust, they began to turn towards them and give chase.

'Come back, you idiots!' I roared furiously as they vanished, because I knew that in that weather they'd never find us again and I'd done enough escorts to know that chasing distant planes helped nobody. Sure enough the Moranes disappeared to the south and we never saw them again, so that I found myself once more the sole escort for the BEs.

Frank was on my right, and Wickitt and I kept exchanging signals.

'Cold,' he said.

'Hungry,' I replied.

'Thirsty.' He lifted his arm as though drinking from a beer bottle.

'Wish I were home,' I replied.

Helped by the strong south-west wind, we made rapid progress. We flew first in a big sweep to the north-east in the hope of misleading the Germans into thinking we were heading for the railway junction at Roulers and also to leave Tourcoing to the south to keep out of the way of the Fokkers that we knew lay in wait there for us. As soon as the first bombs fell, the field telephones would start jangling and they'd know where we'd gone and be across our path on the journey home, together with their friends from Douai, and, now that the Moranes had vanished, I for one wasn't anxious to see them.

We turned over Ledeghem and headed in a southerly and easterly direction, the BEs strung out more and more as the faster machines forged ahead. We reached Avelghelm at last and I saw the BEs assembling over Vaermaerde, then they began to go down one after the other into the murk below the broken cloud and I saw the anti-aircraft shells bursting about them as they dwindled in size. I stayed close to Frank on the approach, and waited just above him as he went in to drop his bombs. I saw the explosions flash on the ground and the lifting mushrooms of smoke, then I climbed up again into the broken cloud to wait for him.

Exhausted by the cold and the wind in my face, I even began to wish some German would try to interfere, just to warm things up a little. Then I realised I was more tired than I'd thought and started to think of leave and all the things I could do when I got home, and slowly began to feel better.

Frank was lifting up again towards me now, his bombs dropped, following the others who by now were beginning to straggle away eastwards again. Wickitt's mouth was opening and shutting and I guessed he was singing.

We were flying south-west now to take the shortest route home, a line that would carry us midway between the dangerous areas of Tourcoing and Douai, and as we headed into the teeth of the wind, the speed of the BEs fell almost to nothing. Flying to one side, I could see Wickitt with his head bent against the gale, crouched over his map, as they followed the others eastwards. They seemed to be falling farther and farther behind, I noticed, and then I saw spurts of blue smoke coming from the exhausts and realised they were having trouble with their engine. Watching them anxiously, I edged closer, praying that their faltering machine would keep going until they could glide to safety beyond the lines.

After a while there was a flurry of rain from the second level of cloud that lay at an unimaginable height above us, and for a moment it blotted out the sky. When it stopped I saw that several of the

BEs had turned north towards Ypres as though to avoid the worst of the weather.

They drew away rapidly, only four of them remaining with me, and for a moment I wondered which ones I was supposed to escort. If only those lunatics in the Moranes had stayed with us, I thought, they could have looked after one lot and I could have looked after the other.

I hadn't a chance of catching up with the northern group and in the end I decided to stay with Frank and Wickitt. I knew them best and they still appeared to be having trouble with their engine. As I edged in closer, Frank lifted his head and grinned at me. Then he moved his arm in one of our prearranged signals. 'Cold,' he was saying.

'Home soon,' I replied.

We were still busy signalling when I saw the brown Fokker appear against the clouds above us. I didn't know where he'd come from but he was turning and had already begun a long glide down.

'Here we go,' I thought. We'd had more good luck than we were entitled to, and here came our share of bad.

I got into position behind and above Frank, and the Fokker came down in a long flat dive into the middle of the other three machines just ahead which scattered wildly and set off for home in different directions. The Fokker pulled up, as though the pilot didn't know which one to attack first, and I opened the throttle and went for him as fast as I could. My gun was working well and, frightening him away by shooting at long range, I turned back towards Frank and Wickitt. But as I swung round I saw there were *two* Fokkers and the second was hovering just above Frank's BE. We weren't the only people who'd worked out tactics. Obviously the first Fokker had come down to lure me away from my straggler so that it was left free for the second.

Desperately, shouting a hopeless warning, I heaved the DH round. I was still higher than the second Fokker, but I was too far away by this time to help and I saw Frank watching me and, unaware of the danger, still flying straight and level; and the Fokker pilot behind, steadying his machine to shoot.

'Frank!' I screamed. 'Behind you!'

His face was still turned towards me, however, and I could see Wickitt with his head down in the cockpit. I waved frantically and pointed.

Frank seemed to think I was just passing the time of day and waved back and raised his hand to his mouth as though having a drink. I could almost see what he was thinking. 'Leave now! Plenty to eat and drink and plenty of girls!'

I saw the Fokker turn away and knew it had fired, and I held my breath, praying he'd missed. But I saw the BE lurch and knew he hadn't. It seemed to lose flying speed, then I saw that Wickitt was kneeling up on his seat, firing away back at the Fokker over Frank's head. But the BE was already sliding off on one wing and I watched it lose height in a spiral as I roared down. Even as I approached, I saw a piece fall off the right upper wing, then the whole wing-tip tore away and went fluttering down.

The BE was already mortally stricken and it lurched away in a sideslip, just as I passed it. Frank seemed to see me and give me a despairing look; then, to my horror, the wings folded back with a bang I could hear even above my own engine.

I saw Frank's arms go up to protect himself from the fabric and spars that were collapsing about his head, then the nose dropped and the machine fell like the stick of a spent rocket, its front end dragged down by the heavy engine, the tail wagging slightly with the speed of its fall.

For a moment, I watched, shocked and disbelieving as it vanished between the scattering of cloud, and saw the sudden glow of flame as it struck the ground.

'Frank,' I said out loud. 'Oh, Frank!'

I felt desperate and alone. I had known Frank all my life and it was like losing a limb and I found myself talking aloud to myself.

'He's all right. He's all right.' I was trying to persuade myself. 'He got out of it. Perhaps it didn't happen.'

But it had and I knew it had, and I remembered numbly what Geoffrey had said – ages ago now, it seemed – 'Sometimes it's not the man next to you who gets hurt, it's *you*!' The war, to which we'd gone so expectant of glory, had turned out differently from what any of us had imagined and it had been Frank and Wickitt and Geoffrey himself who'd found out the truth of his words.

The Fokker's dive had carried it past me now and it had joined its companion to harass the remaining BEs. I was still above them, going down on them now with the DH shuddering with its speed. The

Fokker which had killed Frank was in front of me, moving away to the left as though it was sliding, with that curious crablike motion an aeroplane not on the same course always has in the air, and I moved the stick slightly to bring my sights on to him. In my fury I went in as close as I could, determined to avenge Frank. The Fokker was still two hundred yards away, then a hundred and fifty, a hundred, fifty, forty, thirty, until it seemed to fill the whole sky.

I was firing now and I smelled cordite and heard the gun clattering and saw it jumping in the mount. The Fokker loomed as large as a house in front of me, a brown-and-grey-speckled machine with an engine cowling that looked like the hand-hammered pewter of my mother's kitchen teapot. The pilot's head turned and I saw a wire come loose from that pyramid above his head, then I had to pull away wildly because I thought I was going to fly, still shooting, right into his cockpit.

As I swung aside, missing his wing-tip by what seemed inches, I turned below him and saw he was going down rapidly. Pieces were dropping off the tail and his propeller had stopped and there was a lot of blue smoke coming from underneath the engine. I stared in amazement, startled by what I'd done in red rage and was almost inclined to shout 'Sorry' across the intervening space for damaging his beautiful aeroplane in my temper.

The pilot seemed to have disappeared into the cockpit and, as the Fokker lifted slightly, I saw his head was down, almost out of sight. The Fokker passed me so close I felt I could have touched it, then it went down in a steep glide towards the earth, passing me in a wide arc.

For a moment I lost him, but I caught sight of him again, moving across the earth, still trailing a blue streamer of smoke, then it came to an abrupt stop and a red spot glowed, no more than a mile from where the other fire still burned.

Stupefied, I lifted my head, suddenly realising what I'd done. While I'd been watching, the other Fokker could have killed me, but he'd seen what had happened to his friend and had bolted for home and I could see him now, heading eastwards in a long slanting dive.

The BEs seemed to have disappeared altogether now and I was alone in the ragged sky, still staring, shocked and wretched, at that long winding trail of blue smoke hanging in the air.

Two days later I went home on leave. I was still a bit dazed, still living within myself, still finding it hard to accept that Frank and Wickitt were dead.

When we'd landed everyone had congratulated me on destroying the Fokker, carefully refraining from mentioning the fact that there were two empty chairs in the mess at dinner. I'd hardly heard them, preoccupied still with what I'd done.

I seemed to have found the answer to the whole business of aerial combat at last. It was useless hanging around at a distance of a hundred yards. For the first time, in a rage, I'd gone in really close and the Fokker had fallen out of the sky at once. It had seemed so simple I was staggered. But what good would it do? I was still shocked that three men had had to die to find out how to do it and was nagged by the uneasy knowledge that, having found out, others, too, would die.

I'd waited for hours near the C.O.'s telephone, hoping against hope that it would ring and there'd be a message to say that Frank and Wickitt had escaped the crash and reached safety. In my heart of hearts, though, I'd known all along it couldn't ever be so.

That evening Frank's death was confirmed and the C.O. told me to pack his kit and take the tender the following morning to the railhead and the train to the coast.

I went through Frank's belongings, packing them carefully for return to his parents, then I rolled up his bedding and arranged for the stores to pick it up. I kept his pocket watch, which he'd always hung on a nail above his bed, and a silver cigarette case which I think had belonged to his grandfather, deciding I'd post them home from England, then I wrote a letter to his parents and one to Wickitt's. They were painful, sad letters that I found hard to write. When I'd finished them I began to wonder again what it was all about.

Under normal circumstances we'd just about this time have been leaving school, but, as it was, Frank was dead and I'd killed a man in combat a couple of miles above the earth.

I went off the following morning before dawn and slept all the way to the coast. I woke to find I'd been asleep leaning against an elderly colonel. As I started to wakefulness, full of profuse apologies, he smiled and offered me a cigarette.

'That's all right, my boy,' he said. 'Have a cigarette.'

'I don't smoke,' I told him.

At Calais we followed the Military Police on to the ferry. I was still unable to shut out of my mind that picture of the German aeroplane going down to destruction, and Frank and Wickitt hurtling to their deaths at a speed that would dig their own grave.

I found a seat out of the wind and slept all the way to Dover where I managed to send a telegram to say I was coming home. I hadn't realised how tired I was, but I stared blank-eyed out of the window all the way to London. Victoria was full of women waiting to welcome their menfolk home.

I caught a taxi across London to Liverpool Street Station, and sat frowning heavily all the way to Norwich. At Norwich I changed on to the local line and jerked and shook in the rattling little carriage until the train stopped at Fynling.

I climbed out of the train slowly, pulling my kit after me. There was a cold wind blowing, but the sun was shining, clear and bright in a sign of spring, and I could see the marshes stretching as far as the eye could travel to the North Sea. The stationmaster whom I'd known as a boy nodded to me.

''Mornin', Master Martin,' he said. 'Nice to see you 'ome safe and sound.'

I looked round at the empty platform and, faintly resentful that no one had bothered to meet me, I went out of the station, still desperately trying to shut out of my mind that picture of Frank raising his arms to ward off the collapsing wing of his machine and then that swift descent to oblivion and the glow of flames at the end of it. Now, with the sound of motors silent, it seemed a long time ago and far away.

I blinked rapidly, trying to force it aside. There was a pony and trap standing by the station entrance, with a girl at the reins, but I didn't know her and I turned away towards the village in the hope of getting a lift home from the grocer's van.

'Hello, Martin!'

The voice was familiar and as I turned I realised that the girl in the trap was Jane. She'd had her hair cut short and, instead of the woollen stockings I'd always known, she was wearing silk ones. She looked fresh and clean and calm, and, above all, kind.

'Hello, Janey!'

She smiled. 'Thought I'd bring the trap down to meet you,' she said. 'I've been waiting a long time because, of course, typical of you, you said you were coming but didn't say which train.'

I threw my bag into the trap and climbed up beside her. She looked sharply at me.

'You all right?' she asked. 'You look rotten.'

'Just tired,' I said. 'That's all.'

She was still looking at me, frowning, suspecting something had happened.

'Where's Frank?' she said. 'Didn't he come with you?'

I shook my head. 'Frank won't be coming home,' I said shortly.

She stared at me for a moment, then she seemed to understand what I was trying to tell her.

'Oh!'

For a moment she was silent, sitting motionless with her hands on her lap, holding the reins and the whip, then she seemed to jerk herself back to the present and spoke briskly.

'I expect you're hungry,' she said in an unnecessarily loud voice. 'Better come to our place. Your mother's at the hospital and your father finally got himself involved with the war. He's away most of the time. I'll get you a meal.'

She was brisk, informative and no-nonsense, and I was immensely grateful. I couldn't have stood anything else just then.

'Thanks, Janey,' I said.

She whipped up the pony and we began to bowl along the road away from the station. I was terribly reminded of when Geoffrey was killed and of her feeling then that getting on with something was the only way to approach tragedy.

'Blossom's out,' she said in matter-of-fact tones that forced me to pay attention. 'Do they have blossom in France?'

I made an effort under her goading to pull myself together. 'Yes,' I said. 'Bigger than this, though. Everything's bigger in France. Mice like cats. Cats like horses.'

She turned, startled, and she must have realised how much I'd put into the effort, because she stared at me for a moment and leaned over, swaying to the movement of the trap, to peck my cheek.

'It's nice to have you home, Martin,' she said. Then straightening up, almost as though nothing had happened, she turned and gave her attention to the pony.

Her gesture lifted my heart and I wondered why I'd never noticed before how pretty she was. I felt better already. I was pleased to be with her and enormously grateful to be in England again.